A Necromancer Called Gam Gam

Chronicles of Gam Gam Book One

Adam Holcombe

BOUNTY INK PRESS

Also by Adam Holcombe

Chronicles of Gam Gam

A Necromancer Called Gam Gam
The Wishing Stone

Bounty Inc

Bounty Inc (Coming 2025)

A Necromancer Called Gam Gam

Chronicles of Gam Gam
Book One

Adam Holcombe

BOUNTY INK PRESS

bountyink.com

To Sarah.
My endless pillar of support.
My stories wouldn't be here without you.
I love you.

1

Mina fled from the dread and the pain. From the nightmare and the sorrow. From the barking of hounds and the shouts of murderers. The silence of the forest amplified the sounds of her bare feet into an explosion of noise, sending up echoes of the snapping of twigs and crackling of leaves. She ran recklessly through the darkness, bouncing between the trees before crashing to the ground. Her momentum clawed her back to sore, raw feet. Her heart pounded against the prison of her rib cage; her gasping breath left a moist film on her lips that she kept rubbing away. Still she continued, branches clawing at her bare arms like giant beasts reaching out from the dark. The cool autumn air chilled the sweat against her body almost as quickly as it appeared. Mina wished she'd grabbed her coat and shoes. She wished for a lot of things.

A single flickering light called through the shroud of night. A traveler? She could only hope to be so lucky as to find a valiant knight. But would anyone even help her? The howls of the dogs grew louder, urging Mina toward that beacon. She pushed on with what little hope dwelled in her chest and focused on that single light as it grew into a flame, then a fire. The bright embers burned her eyes and deepened the darkness around her. With a resounding thud, Mina slammed into a tree and bounced off it, barely able to keep her footing as she stumbled backward.

Gingerly, she touched her bruised bicep. She winced at the pain, her breaths still coming ragged and fast, and she took in the sight ahead of her: a small camp with a fire at its heart. A solitary silhouette sat in a chair near the flames, arms shifting in repeated motion. A large, hard-topped wagon stood at the light's edge. The sort merchants sold goods from when they visited the village. Beyond, two horses lay, strangely unmoving, beneath the boughs of a tree.

From behind, the barking echoed through the forest. The silhouette shifted, and Mina ducked behind the tree. Her pursuers were so close; she was so tired. And cold. Violent shivers wracked her body and begged her for that fire. Her legs and feet were beyond pain now; only a dull numbness told her they were still attached. Her lungs felt raw, like they'd been pulled from her body and scraped against a washboard. She wanted to give up. She wanted warmth. If she could just sit by the fire for a few moments, she could stop the shaking.

When she peeked around the edge of the tree, the figure had turned back toward the flames, their arms moving in that same mesmerizing motion. Her gaze shifted to the wagon, and it called to her with promises of warmth and safety. The fire wasn't her only option. She might find clothes in the wagon. A blanket.

Guilt choked her, but fear pushed her. Introductions were not an option. She was wanted, and she was a killer. If the silhouetted person didn't hand her over, they would seize her with force. She couldn't risk asking for help, but she had to risk helping herself.

She tiptoed toward the wagon, carefully stepping between twigs and leaves. Her legs burned at the slow process, the different motion stretching taut muscles until they were sure to snap. *Breathe.* She had to focus on her breathing, as her father taught her, let it calm her nerves and relax her body. She couldn't afford to panic right now. Her eyes jumped from the ground to the silhouette, who sat as before, arms working tirelessly. Mina reached the rear doors of the wagon, and she hoped the hinges were recently greased. She glanced at the horses and noticed they were not even tied to a stake or tree. Another burst of anxiety and guilt warred within her. If the hounds pursuing her scared the horses away, the traveler would be stranded. It would be her fault.

The voices shouted, near enough that Mina could hear the words. She was out of time. She took a deep breath and grabbed one of the door handles, barely feeling the cold metal in her numb hands. She cracked it open enough to fit through, and the hinges were so silent, Mina almost cried out in relief. She crept within and pulled the door partially closed behind her, leaving it open just enough to see and hear clearly.

The light of the fire bisected the otherwise dark abyss within. Mina's teeth chattered as her body came to rest, the heat of exercise no longer staving off the fierce chill that pierced her skin. She groped around and felt something soft and heavily textured and pulled it close. With the dull light, she noticed the shape and several patterns stitched throughout. A blanket! She wrapped the new-found woolen blanket around herself quickly. Warmth returned, enough that her violent shaking subsided. Her skin still prickled, and her feet were numb, but those too would recover, given time.

The hounds' snarls and the soldiers' hails announced their arrival as they burst from the woods. Mina knelt near the door and peered out, but no one entered her minimal frame of vision.

"Hello, boys. I didn't expect any visitors tonight, especially not this late." An elderly woman's voice reached Mina. Was she traveling alone? Was she not afraid to do so? "Is there anything I can help you with?"

A gruff voice answered, words curt and precise. "We're looking for a girl: sable-skinned, shoulder-length, black hair. Approximately twelve years of age. Have you seen her run this way?"

"I have not—excuse me! What are you doing?" The old lady's voice shifted from calm, pleasant tones to scolding within a heartbeat.

"We must check your wagon in case she hid within." The dogs pawed at the ground, their claws scraping against stone and dirt. Mina could imagine them, saliva dripping from their jaws as they pulled against their restraints, instincts drawing them toward her like beasts to their next meal. She supposed she was meant to be the meal. "The dogs seem to believe she's this way. You should be careful. There are things worse than thieves in these woods. I'd hate for someone your age to run into anything terrible."

"It seems I already have." The woman's voice grew closer as she continued speaking. "It is not the thief who sneaks in the night that I am worried about. It's the brutes who push and bully to get their way."

"Ma'am, I assure you, it will be a quick inspection. Nothing to worry about."

"And I assure you, you will need more men if you wish to illegally search my wagon."

"It is not illegal. I have the power vested in me by the Eternal Empire to search anywhere with reasonable—"

"Baked goods," the old woman interrupted.

"What?"

"It is likely your hounds smell my baked goods. I have a small oven within and finished baking some chocolate chip scones not that long ago. I will not have you ransacking my home because you do not feed your animals properly. Now, if you'll leave me be, I was in the middle of something very important."

The footsteps around the wagon halted, though the dogs' paws continued to scrape against the ground in an effort to reach their target. Mina slid away from the door, heart beating faster than it had while she was running through the woods. One old lady would not prevent them from entering, not when the dogs smelled her. They would open the wagon and drag her out, and she would—

Mina bumped a stack of crates, sending something clattering to the ground. She stilled, straining to listen outside. The conversation continued, its participants unaware. She was about to breathe again when the clattering continued, snaking its way around the wagon like little claws clacking against the wood. Closer and closer it came to her, and she tucked her legs in tight as the sound darted past her. She bit down hard on one hand to halt the scream that filled her throat. Her eyes opened wide, pulling in all the light they could find as she looked through the wagon, but the dark was much too thick. As suddenly as the clattering started, it came to a stop somewhere nearby, out of sight. For long moments, the wagon was silent again. Mina tried convincing herself that something had just fallen and rolled around, that her mind was playing tricks on her. It was enough to get herself breathing again. One breath at a time.

"We act under the power of the Eternal Empire, and we will be forced to restrain you if you do not cooperate."

Mina had missed something in the conversation. They were close now, just on the other side of the door. She heard the dogs scraping at the ground and pictured the slobber flying from their jaws as they barked.

Breathe.

She closed her eyes and pulled the blanket tighter. Calm is what she needed now. Despite everything, she needed to find peace within herself. There was one thing she could do, though she had promised never to do it again. But this was an emergency, and she doubted the precautions mattered anymore. They were meant to protect her, and they had failed. Maybe her cursed power would succeed instead.

The feeling thrummed at the back of her mind, a valve ready to be released and fill her with pulsating energy. The conversation continued outside, the woman arguing to no avail. They would be stalled only so long; it was two—four if you counted the dogs—against one, and she would surely be overpowered. When she was, they would not find Mina within. She opened her eyes, letting the wealth of power fill her limbs, burning warmth back into them. Then she pushed—

The growls turned to whimpers, the whimpers into whining. Fear infected the hounds, and their yelping broke Mina's concentration. Her power fled, leaving her body devoid of the buzzing energy, and the chill renewed its assault. Mina crawled to the door, and through the gap, she could just make out a dog, its tail curved between its legs. It yelped and howled as if it were being beaten, but the soldier holding its leash only looked at it in confusion and anger. It fought against its handler, pulling him off balance. The dog was desperate to reach the woods, to be as far away from the wagon as possible. Obscenities were hurled at the hound like stones, but still it tugged.

Mina could hear the other dog, and though she couldn't see, its voice told much the same story.

What is happening?

"Blasted mutt! What's wrong with you?" The soldier pulled hard on the leash, enough to jerk the dog back and onto its side. Its limbs flailed in the air for a moment, its fearful howling ceaseless. Then it was on its feet again, and it bolted with what slack the leash allowed. Caught unprepared, the leash tore from the man's hand, and the dog disappeared into the night.

The man stared after the dog for a moment; his face bloomed red, though Mina wasn't sure if it was colored by anger or embarrassment. He looked at his companion, but before the other soldier could say anything, the first man bolted into the night after the runaway hound, obscenities once more his useless weapon of choice.

"Oh my, they seem so frightened," the old woman said, sounding unworried.

The remaining soldier yelled after his retreating companion, his own dog pulling hard against its lead. "These mutts are worth a fortune. He better not—"

The words died in his mouth, and Mina saw a flash of shadow as the second dog gave chase to the first. How had that one gotten loose? Mina shifted within the wagon, risking noise to get a better angle. The soldier stood near the doors, only a few steps away. He stared at something beyond the wagon, beyond where the woman's voice originated. His face was pale as moonlight.

"What in the hells?" he mumbled.

"Run."

The single word scared Mina more than anything else that night. It seeped like an ooze through the cracks of the wagon's walls, coating her in a film of fear as the boards beneath her vibrated as if to escape that horrible sound. A shockwave of terror emanated from that single word, and Mina felt tears form in her eyes at the thought of facing the owner of that voice.

The man had no walls to hide behind, so his tears ran freely. His limbs locked in place, face frozen in a mask of fear. Then his knees buckled. The collision with the ground seemed to send a wave of sense up to his brain, and the startled soldier scrambled back to his feet and charged after his companion.

Mina's own limbs locked beneath her; despite the blanket, she shook uncontrollably. She could hide from the men, maybe even from the dogs. But whatever was out there now, it was sure to kill the old woman and her next. Mina's powers couldn't stop something like that. Not when a single word could send a soldier running. Not when she was so far from calm.

Mina trembled beneath the blanket, her mind spinning in circles. Hide. She had to stay here. Maybe it wouldn't check the wagon. Maybe—

"Thank you, dear. Those two were certainly trouble."

Mina froze. Surely the woman wasn't speaking to her—

"You're very welcome, my lady," a smooth, resonant voice responded. It was the same voice that had told the soldier to run, Mina could tell that much. But different now, laced with kindness instead of horror. "I shall run them in circles for a bit to tire them."

"Make sure to drop them off somewhere not too unpleasant."

"Of course, my lady."

Mina listened for the retreating footsteps that never came. The speaker was silent as a wolf treading through the woods—if he had moved at all. She would have to wait longer to ensure he had departed. Then she would—

"You can come out now. Everyone's gone."

Mina stiffened, her breath caught midway to her lungs. She waited, wondering if the woman was speaking to someone else again.

After a long pause, the old woman continued, "Or you can stay in there if you wish." There was no doubt these comments were directed at Mina now. "Try not to harm Nugget please. He's a good boy, despite his looks."

Nugget?

Mina shivered as a tentative, single clack sounded in the wagon. She turned her head. A small, porcelain-white face stared at her, black holes for eyes, bared, sharp teeth shining bright in the sliver of light. Mina failed to hold back the yelp this time, and as she jumped away from the creature, she fell into the door, which swung open at her sudden impact and deposited her roughly onto the ground in a puff of dirt and grunt of pain.

A cat, free from the restraints of flesh, muscle, and organ, stretched on the edge of the wagon, as if that would do anything for its skeletal body. Then it jumped down next to Mina and plodded over to the woman, who had returned to her chair by the fire. A partially-knitted scarf coiled in her lap as she continued to work on it. The skeletal cat found a comfortable piece of the woman's dress, curled up at her feet, and licked its non-existent crotch with a non-existent tongue.

"I don't have another chair, but there was a log over there that didn't look too pokey that you could use as a seat."

Mina stood, blanket still draped around her shoulders, and walked toward the fire, drawn by its heat. She stopped short, and tremors ran through her limbs at the denial of warmth. "How do you know I'm not evil?"

"I have learned in my time that if two men are chasing a young girl, it is never the girl's fault." The woman looked up from her knitting and smiled at Mina. Her pale skin was painted orange by the firelight, but her purple eyes sparkled. She was even older than Mina had originally thought. Wrinkles gathered in crowds around her eyes and mouth. Her hair was whiter than the moon. She had to be ancient.

"My father's dead because of me." Mina was surprised at the words. Not because of what they said, but because they had been spoken at all. Her throat constricted, and a heat burned behind her eyes. Yet the words continued. "Killers aren't good people."

The old lady set her knitting down in her lap, her expression turning somber. "How was it your fault, dear?"

"Those soldiers, they work for a man. He wants me for my..." Tears rolled down both cheeks, and she brushed them away quickly. She didn't want the stranger to think her a baby. "He just wants me, and he killed my father to get me. It's my fault." Now the tears came in earnest, and she couldn't stop them. She shoved her face into the blanket and fought against the sobs that rose in her throat. She failed.

Two arms reached around Mina and pulled her into a tight embrace, engulfing her in the many layers of the woman's dress. Shock halted Mina's tears, and she lifted her head from the blanket and looked up at the woman.

"That's not evil, dear. That's your father's love." She brushed a loose hair back from Mina's face. "You remind me so much of my dear granddaughter. Evelyn put too much on her shoulders just as you are doing now. Those two men, and the one who ordered them, are the *only* ones responsible for what happened. The actions of others are never your fault."

Mina broke.

Grief and exhaustion overwhelmed her. She cried into the dress of the kind stranger until her tears dried up. Her voice fled from her in great, heaving sobs until it cracked and turned to coughing. And the woman held her for as long as Mina needed to be held. A few minutes or a few hours, she did not know. All she knew was the black pit of despair that hollowed out a place within her. It hurt worse than her bruised and cut feet. Worse than her scraped knees. So much worse than any pain she had felt before.

When Mina's cheeks were sticky with drying tears and her breathing had settled into something more controlled, the woman led her to the not-too-pokey log. She provided Mina with half of a meat pie and two chocolate chip scones—all immediately devoured—and she cleaned and bandaged Mina's feet. The woman found a large pair of boots in her wagon and stuffed them with cloth until they almost fit Mina's much smaller feet.

The warmth from the flames and the food rushed to meet each other and drove the shivering from Mina's body. The boots and the blankets trapped the heat within her, and for the first time since her father died, the chill departed.

The woman introduced herself as Gam Gam and offered Mina a place to sleep within her wagon. Mina cried again that night—soft, silent tears—before she fell asleep with Gam Gam's soft breaths to one side of her and Nugget curled up on the other.

Fatherless and on the run, Mina wasn't sure what was to come in the days ahead of her. But Fate had a way of finding the right person at the right time, and Fate had found her Gam Gam. She would never have guessed how much Gam Gam would need her as well.

Mina woke from one nightmare to another. She clung to her blanket as she gasped for air, throat raw though she didn't remember screaming. Nugget scrambled away and, once he reached a safe distance, glared at her. As much as a skeletal cat can glare, anyway. Mina looked around for Gam Gam, but the older woman was absent from the wagon. There was certainly nowhere she could be hiding. Anxiety roiled within Mina's stomach, and last night's dinner rose within her, threatening to escape. She clutched her stomach and gritted her teeth, holding down the wave of nausea.

If Gam Gam wasn't in the wagon, then she was outside. If the soldiers returned, they might have found her. The dogs knew where she was; they could find her again. They might be out there already, slavering over her scent, waiting to spring... Mina drew in a shaky breath and pushed the thought away–or tried. It lingered, needling at her mind.

If they returned, Gam Gam could be—

"Are you awake, dear?" Gam Gam called from outside. "I thought I heard Nugget clattering around."

Mina's breath expelled, her heart settled into a steadier rhythm, and her hands stilled. Her whole body stilled. She regained control of herself and wiped the sweat, or maybe it was tears, from her face. She shut her eyes and breathed in deeply, then out. Gam Gam was fine, and Mina had survived a night. She could survive another. "Yeah," she said.

"Excellent. Food will be warming over the fire whenever you're ready to eat," the elderly woman called. "Hope you like eggs and potatoes. I don't have much else for food until our next stop, but I may have some sausages that haven't gone bad yet if you'd like to risk it."

"Eggs and potatoes are fine." Gratitude overwhelmed Mina, and with it more tears. She cried over something as dumb as breakfast, but she couldn't stop herself. Mina sniffed and wiped her face dry. Belatedly, she added, "Thank you!"

"You're welcome, dear. There's a cloak hanging on the door. It'll be big on you, but it should keep you plenty warm until we can get you something that fits."

The daylight illuminated the interior from two long windows on her right. Mina found the cloak, a simple garment of brown cloth with purple flowers embroidered along the sleeves. But before she draped it over herself, Mina took a moment to look around the brightened wagon for the first time.

It was large, larger than she had realized previously. Wide enough that four more people could have slept next to Mina, and none of them would have been touching. Long enough that she could pace several times before having to turn. But there would be no pacing or turning, not with the quantity of *things*. All sorts of things. Crates, sacks, and chests lined the walls and stood in precarious stacks. Many appeared to be filled with perishables, others with clothing. But a vast majority were filled with yarn, either in skeins or already knitted into scarves, mittens, sweaters, and countless other garments. It was an unreasonable amount of yarn.

Opposite the windows, a small stove was built into the wall, its chimney jutting out the top of the wagon. The stove was cold, but given the clutter, much of it flammable (not even taking into account the wooden walls, floor, and ceiling), Mina was sure that was for the best. Gam Gam's scones were delicious, but she wasn't sure they were worth losing home and life over!

Mina pulled herself to her feet, and pain flared across her soles and up her legs. Her hand grabbed at a large chest to steady herself, and she bit down hard on her lip to stop from crying out. Her breath came in a rapid pulse as she carefully stretched to work out the worst of the cramping and aches. The pain dulled as she took unsteady steps around the wagon, though the unpleasant soreness and burning remained. Walking away from the doors, toward the wagon's front, Mina noticed a large hatch in the wall in front of her, which appeared able to slide to one side. She suspected opening it would reveal a driver's bench on the other side, though what the hatch was used for was lost on Mina. It was awkwardly high to grab anything from the seat, at least not without falling in.

Mina shrugged, and feeling confident enough she wouldn't topple, she pulled the large cloak on. The ends brushed the ground like a ballroom dress, and her hands reached two-thirds of the way to the sleeves' ends, but Gam Gam was right about its warmth. She pushed the doors open and gently lowered herself onto the ground. Strong, savory smells wafted to her as Mina approached the fire. Her stomach roared in excitement.

Gam Gam filled a plate and handed it over, smiling as bright as the morning sun. Mina took the plate with a small smile of her own, thanked her, then took up her seat on the not-too-pokey log and began eating. Gam Gam filled her own plate and ate from her chair. A silence drifted with the fire smoke between them as they ate, but something about Gam Gam's presence made it comforting.

The first bites melted in Mina's mouth with delicious flavor. Her papa did all the cooking back home—though Mina would help with baking pumpkin seeds occasional-ly—so she wasn't sure *how* Gam Gam did it, but it was one of the greatest meals Mina had ever tasted. It took her a few more bites before she realized she was scarfing the meal down in a way that often made her papa laugh and call her "Little Piggy." Mina forced herself to slow down and glanced at Gam Gam to see if she was offended. The elderly woman paid Mina no heed as she watched the flames dance and picked at her food.

Beyond Gam Gam, Mina caught sight of the two horses she had seen the previous night. They stood still, staring out into the woods. Their tails flicked occasionally, but otherwise neither moved. Mina was glad to find they had not been scared off by the hounds, or whatever else had shown up.

"Do they have names?" Mina asked as she bit down on a small, round potato. It burst in her mouth as the skin tore, the inside soft and mushy.

"Hmm?" Gam Gam looked away from the fire, then traced Mina's gaze. "Oh! The horses, yes. The gray one on the right is Sebastian. The brown and black one is Nora. They're a feisty pair, however, and they love the taste of fingers, so beware. But they get me to where I need to go and do a great job of it."

Mina, who happened to be a big fan of her fingers, took note to keep her distance from the nibbly horses. Gam Gam returned to picking at her plate. The silence resumed, and when Gam Gam finished first, a much smaller helping on her own plate than Mina's, she placed the cleared dish in a bucket inside the wagon. She told Mina to do the same, and to not bother cleaning it right now. Dishes could be done when it started getting dark. Daylight was for travel.

Gam Gam continued clearing the campsite as Mina finished eating. The old woman was efficient, and by the time Mina's dish hit the bucket, both horses were hooked up to their harnesses, and the wagon was ready to depart.

At the wagon's front, a single step led to an oak bench that ran the width. So, there was plenty of room for seating, though Mina stuck closely to one side as her fingers twisted the excess fabric of her cloak. Gam Gam closed up the wagon, then joined her. She set a small cloth bag at her feet and, as she settled in, pulled out a partial scarf with a pair of needles attached. Mina's brow crinkled at the thought of trying to knit and drive a wagon at the same time. Her eyes nearly popped out when the wagon jolted to a start without a touch of the reins or a word of command.

Despite their desire to bite, Sebastian and Nora turned out to be incredibly well-trained horses. They never wavered from the path as they headed south and never made a noise more than the crunch of leaves and twigs. It was all the more impressive as Gam Gam continued to leave the reins untouched, wrapped around the front guard. Mina had never seen horses act in such a way, almost as if they understood Gam Gam's wishes without any commands. Admittedly, Mina hadn't interacted with many horses, so maybe they were more intelligent than she had thought.

As they cleared the small path and merged onto the main road, the sun poured down on them, unabated by the forest's trees. The scarf's colors flashed in the new intense lights, sparkling with a mix of peach, white, and pink. Even hints of blue and green poked out, though Mina could not track where they originated from. The two needles clacked together in a spirited determination to knit the yarn.

Mina's gaze slid out to the road and the surrounding scenery, watching closely for any movement. A sick worry churned her stomach, turning her breakfast sour. What if those soldiers were hidden in the woods, waiting for her? What if they returned and in greater numbers? The wind picked up, and Mina pulled the sizable cloak tighter around herself to fend off the chill.

"Is there anywhere I can take you?" Gam Gam asked, glancing over for a moment before turning back to her knitting. "Any family or friends?"

Mina shook her head, then, realizing Gam Gam's eyes were on her knitting, she spoke quickly. "No. My... My mother's not around. It was just Papa and me." Her stomach twisted and flipped, threatening to reacquaint her with breakfast to see if it tasted as good the second time. She shrugged. "You can just drop me off wherever." She hoped "wherever" was at least away from the soldiers.

"Oh, nonsense, dear. If you have nowhere to go then there is nowhere you *will* go." Gam Gam paused her knitting to smile at Mina. "You're welcome to my company for as long as you can handle it. I'm heading west to the sea. There's a beautiful cliff that you can watch the sunset from. Would you like to see it?"

Mina's emotions went to war within her, happiness and sadness squeezing at her heart while fear and excitement sent sparks through her head. Maybe if she traveled far enough, no one would be looking for her. But... *West*. Angry cramps squeezed at her stomach, and Mina had to focus on her breathing. East would be better. Away, not toward.

She bit her lip and nodded. She had no other choice and did not wish to inconvenience Gam Gam. She tried to sound happy as she said, "Sure," but Gam Gam didn't look convinced.

"Wonderful," Gam Gam said with a warm, comforting smile that Mina was growing to love. Mina tried her own smile, though it was no more than a shell of the older woman's.

Gam Gam's gaze jerked upward from her knitting and focused on something far ahead. Mina looked but could only see a few wagons stopped on the road and the faint shapes of people. Could Gam Gam really see so much better?

"You should climb into the wagon," Gam Gam said, her tone shifting from cheery to worried. "Through the window here." She unlatched and slid open the hatch without a look back.

"Why? Is something wrong?"

"Just a precaution, dear. Nothing to worry about."

"Is it more soldiers?"

Gam Gam sighed and turned to Mina. "It might be, but don't worry. Okay? I'll take care of them. I'll keep you safe." Gam Gam placed a hand on Mina's cheek and smiled again. "I promise. Just stay hidden."

Mina hesitated as she looked again at the stopped wagons. Then she climbed through the hatch as her panic pulsed through her body in waves. Her feet hit something soft and unsteady, and she sprawled into a pile. Something jabbed her in the ribs, and a clattering noise filled the wagon as items spilled away from Mina's flailing limbs. The window slid shut behind her, followed by the snap of the latch locking. The bundle of bones at the top of the stove raised its feline skull and looked at Mina, then disregarded her and returned to a nap. Why did skeletal cats need so many naps?

"I didn't need help anyway," Mina said, then she kicked herself free of one pile of stuff and pushed away another pile of things. She was sure an orange burst beneath one oversized boot right before she crashed the other through a small crate. More yarn clung to her even as she plucked free what was already there. By the time she cleared enough space to sit, her legs burned from the effort, and she collapsed to the floor. Then she waited.

The cart slowed to a stop, then rolled forward and stopped again. And again. And again. The final time it stopped, Mina heard snippets of conversation sneak through the wooden walls. Gam Gam had reached the front of the line and whatever awaited them there. There was no barking or growling, just the voices of men and women. That meant no dogs. Mina felt a small amount of relief ease her tense muscles. Maybe they weren't here for her, and everything would be fine.

The wagon shifted and creaked as Gam Gam climbed down. Mina focused and could make out the words well enough when she held her breath.

"...inspecting all carts and wagons..." a man said. Mina's muscles tensed again as she took a deep breath to listen.

"...my personal belongings...ruffians searching..." Gam Gam used the same scolding tone as she had the night before.

"...a thief...a sergeant and she...'"

"...no thieves..."

"...only a moment."

The words grew softer. As they rounded the wagon, Gam Gam's voice gave chase. The voices turned sour as an argument formed.

"...you scoundrel! That is..."

"...standard procedure for esc..."

"...sergeant? I want..."

"...inspection is finished. For now..."

The voices reached the wagon's doors.

Gam Gam continued to argue with the guards but seemingly in vain. Panic gripped at Mina, and her heartbeat pulsed through her entire body. She took shallow, quick breaths as her lungs had difficulty handling more. She pulled her cloak tighter and squeezed her eyes shut to the sounds of the door rattling.

They were going to get in. They would search the wagon and find her, huddled like a frightened child in the back. She would be dragged from the wagon and taken to *that* man. Mina bit her lip to stop the tears. Her mind flew from thought to thought faster than she could track. They shouldn't have gone west. She should have left on her own. She messed up because she was weak and stupid. And she would—

A coppery taste filled her mouth and slowed her thoughts. Her heartbeat pulsed in her lip, and a pinprick of blood formed where she bit down too hard. The pain and the blood calmed her, reset her brain. Gam Gam still argued with the guards, who threatened to break into the wagon if Gam Gam didn't unlock the door. She would unlock it. Of course she would. What was Mina compared to Gam Gam's home? There was nowhere to hide. They would see her.

Unless they didn't.

Mina closed her eyes and pushed the voices away. The steady in and out of her breath was her entire world. Calmness battled against the agitation within her. Her papa's techniques came to her with practiced ease. They were necessary to avoid her outbursts, a way to control her power and imprison it within. But she didn't *have* to chain it up.

She returned to that familiar force at the back of her mind. She teased it out and felt the energy thrum through her. The power vibrated within each muscle, filling her with warmth and strength. She had avoided her powers the night before, but she had no choice now.

She reached out, like flexing an untrained, unpracticed muscle. It recoiled for a moment, the fear of discovery holding it back, then she pushed harder, and awareness exploded within her.

The lock clicked, and Mina ignored it.

Presences filled her senses, not quite sight or touch, but she could see and feel them nonetheless. Three of them, but one more comfortable than the others, though it burned hot with passion and fury. Mina reached for that hot coal, the heat of anger washing over her as she did.

The door cracked open, and Mina ignored it.

She brushed against Gam Gam's mind. A single moment. All she needed.

Wagon Interior.

An image rushed to the forefront of her mind, and Mina seized it. It slipped from her mental grip and receded back, but she focused on the image as it faded. Held it in her mind until she had a copy. It became her memory, ready to be used.

The door opened, revealing two guards at the same moment Mina projected the memory around the wagon. Across the walls and the piles of junk, across the stove and Nugget. Most importantly, across herself. She opened her eyes, breath held and muscles tense with expectation. The clutter that had filled the wagon was gone. Most of the items that made it homey were missing. The wagon was bare except for a few essentials. Mina's throat squeezed shut at the realization. Gam Gam's reaction solidified her fear.

The red-faced, elderly woman stopped using her cloth bag as a weapon, and her beratement ceased. Instead, her mouth dropped open in surprise, and her eyes widened as they searched the back of her own wagon, now appearing emptied of all her valuables. Gam Gam knew Mina's secret.

The guards were unaware. One held Gam Gam's arm, his other arm raised in a casual defensive posture to block the bag that no longer struck him. The other peered into the wagon, one foot on the back step. Mina focused on these two and pushed her thoughts of Gam Gam away. The fear of the kindly woman's hatred curdled Mina's stomach and threatened to disrupt her projection. It would be a miracle if she made it through the day without vomiting.

The one guard scanned the wagon, making no effort to step inside. Perhaps he would have if the wagon appeared as it should. But the way he saw it, nearly empty, everything neat, there wasn't anywhere for someone to hide. He let his eyes work for him, and Mina tracked their progress. They paused on her, and time froze. Mina's lungs burned from the effort of holding her breath against the fear of noise. Sweat dripped in front of her eyes, and she let it sting them, not wanting to move. Even Mina's heart paused its frantic rhythm.

Then his eyes continued past, and time hurtled forward. Mina forced herself to breathe, slow and quiet despite her lungs begging for more. It had worked. It had *worked*!

Then it almost didn't. Something shimmered behind the guard, something in the shape of a man with glowing armor. Except that the sun shone *through* him, and his eyes glowed red as rage permeated off him. The surprise jolted Mina's attention, and the grip on the projection nearly slipped.

Then the phantasm was gone. Vanished. If it had moved, she would have seen. Instead, it simply ceased to exist a moment after it formed. No one else noticed. Was she hallucinating? Was it a side effect of her powers?

She was distracted when the doors shut again, the lock clicking into place and the murmurs of conversation shifting. Mina released her hold and panted as the power retreated into her. The clutter returned as the image faded from her mind. She slumped against the wall, exhaustion ambushing her as though filling in the void of her power. Her mind felt like a mush not dissimilar to the potatoes she had eaten earlier. Her head tilted to one side, and her eyelids drooped. She was suddenly so tired. Sleep beckoned her, and she answered its call.

3

A knocking on the hatch jerked Mina awake. She pushed up from the awkward position she'd been in and was treated to aches racing down her neck and back. One hand tingled with numbness, and she shook it awake, grimacing against the pinpricks of pain. A few stretches eased the soreness as memory and dread returned to her.

Her heart was strangled by her fear, and the air she pulled into her lungs found them full to capacity and unable to expand. Mina fumbled her way to the hatch in a dazed stumble, her mind focused only on the orange that had been squashed beneath her boot. She pushed every other thought out of her head as she took hold of the handle and held it for a few labored breaths. Then she slid the hatch open and leaned out.

The bottom lip of the window came even with the bench's seat, and both were just below her armpits. So, with relative ease, Mina crossed her arms and leaned her chin out on them. She watched the horses trotting in unison and let their rhythm control her thoughts. The silence stretched for a long moment, but Mina knew the question would arrive soon.

Gam Gam focused on the idle knitting in her lap as she tapped the needles against one another. "How did you do that?"

"Do what?" Mina put all the innocence she could into that one question.

"I might be old, sweetie, but I'm not senile quite yet. The wagon hasn't been that empty since I first bought it." A moment later, she turned to Mina with a squint. "My things are still back there, right? You didn't somehow get rid of them? I had a lot of valuable yarn."

Mina sighed. If she had more time, she could have chosen a better memory and perhaps fooled Gam Gam too, but she had to work with what she grabbed. And unfortunately, what she grabbed was an early memory of the interior.

"I'm a neuromancer." She breathed the hateful words out. A certain amount of relief came with the admission. She would be left behind, but she didn't have to lie any-more. Gam Gam didn't deserve those lies, not after all she had done to help. Especially not when Mina was a target for the empire, a poison that would one day kill Gam Gam as it had her father and her mother.

"Ah! You can pull memories from others and shape them into illusions." Then Gam Gam did the last thing Mina expected. She continued her knitting as if she hadn't just learned that Mina was a monster. In a thoughtful mumble, she added, "Powerful magic."

Mina was speechless for a moment, unsure what was going through Gam Gam's head. When she couldn't take the silence, she forced her own question out. "Will... will you still take me with you?" Her mouth was so dry as she spoke. "To the sea?"

"Of course, dear. Assuming you still want to go, that is. I won't take you anywhere you don't want to go, and I won't leave you anywhere you don't wish to be." Gam Gam smiled down at her, her expression full of the love and comfort Mina had come to expect. The tension melted from Mina, and tears pricked at her eyes as she stared up at the old woman. She felt a smile form on her own lips. Happiness felt like an impossible dream, and maybe it still was, but in that moment, she was more relaxed than she had been since it all began. Her secret was out, and Gam Gam didn't hate her for it. "But first, I think we ought to deal with this little problem. Can't have interruptions on our trip, can we?"

"Deal with it how, Gam Gam?"

"Those guards told me they're looking for a missing girl. A servant who stole money from a sergeant. If they knew it was a neuromancer they were looking for, they would have known to check for illusions. I suspect there's only one person who knows, yes? The subordinates would want to either kill you out of misplaced fear or capture you for personal gain. So, I think if we deal with this sergeant, we'll put an end to our issue."

Our issue. Mina had thought she was alone after her father died. But a stranger had taken her in, cared for her, and wanted to help. And maybe Gam Gam *could* help. "Mikyal."

"The sergeant?"

Mina nodded. "But what can we do against him? Are you... are you going to kill him?"

"Oh, heavens, no!" Gam Gam blinked, startled at the thought. "Killing is horrific. I think a stern talking to will set him straight."

Mina gaped, but Gam Gam had a smile that said anything was possible. "How can we even get to him? He has so many men."

Gam Gam set her knitting down, then reached into the neckline of her dress and removed a medallion. She pulled it from around her neck and handed it to Mina. It was warm in her hands as she studied it: a pale gray bone disc no larger than Mina's palm with an elegant tree engraved in its center. Eight branches reached out evenly to the edges.

"Do you know what this is?" Gam Gam asked.

"Yeah," Mina said, her eyes wide with wonder. "A mage's medallion." She studied it and noticed a single black circle running along the edge. Her excitement faltered. "You're only first level. So you're not very good."

To Mina's surprise, Gam Gam chuckled. "In some cases that's so. But sometimes it means inexperienced. The two are not always synonymous. I received this three months ago."

"Three months? But you're—" Mina broke off and blushed red when Gam Gam finished for her.

"Old? I'm surprised you noticed," she said with a wink and a laugh. "I had a late start. Do you know what the color means? The black."

"Black means…" Mina didn't remember all the colors of magic, but black was an easy one. A magic almost as taboo as her own. "Necromancy," she breathed.

"Yes." Gam Gam retrieved the medallion and replaced it. Then she took up her knitting once more. "As you can imagine, my magic isn't thought of kindly. We're alike in that way, misunderstood and judged for what we *can* do instead of what we *actually* do. You'll never have to fear that from me, dear."

The trepidation Mina had felt earlier disappeared, and in its place excitement blossomed. "Did you use zombies to scare away those men last night?"

"That was me, actually."

Mina jumped, banging her head against the top of the window, and released a squeal of surprise more than pain. She turned, rubbing the sore spot, and the blood drained from her face. At the opposite end of the bench (vacant only moments prior, Mina was certain) sat a transparent, shimmering man. He was at least as old as Gam Gam, with a beard stretching down his chest. His head was bald except for two tufts of hair sticking out above his ears. He wore a knight's armor emblazoned with the symbol of a swan in flight over the shape of a heart. The sword belted to his waist stabbed through the bench without leaving a mark. Mina couldn't tell the color of his hair, eyes, skin, or armor as it was all shades of gray at best and see through at worst. But Mina recognized parts of him as the thing that had appeared behind the soldier.

"Apologies, young miss, I didn't mean to startle," he said as he bowed his head to her.

"Ah, Sir Gibblet, you've returned," Gam Gam said. "I just finished this scarf as a thank you for your diligent work."

"That is much appreciated, my lady, but as I cannot wear it, I must unfortunately decline."

"Oh, I suppose you can't. You'll just have to pretend, I guess." She held up the scarf in all its glorious whites and pinks.

The knight chuckled and ran a hand through his beard. "It is a truly magnificent scarf. If only you were a hundred years older, and I could have served you in life."

"You're a ghost!" Mina's words finally returned. Gam Gam and the ghost laughed.

"Well, I *am* a necromancer, Mina. Sir Gibblet here has been helping me on my travels. Sir Gibblet, this is our new companion, Mina. She's a neuromancer."

Mina clenched at the blatant admission, but Sir Gibblet seemed not to care. Instead, he bowed to Mina again and said, "It's a pleasure to meet you, Lady Mina. It would be my honor to serve at your side."

Mina thanked him and pulled herself up through the window, seating herself between the necromancer and the necromanced. Nugget followed her out and climbed into her lap. She stroked the cat's spine, surprised at how natural it felt, and said, "I guess that explains Nugget too." Something else clicked as she said it. "The horses?"

"I hear neuromancers can see through illusions, no?"

Mina focused on the horses, her power trickling into her, humming with energy, and something shifted in how she saw the horses. Their skin faded until translucent. The harnesses mimicked fitting the illusory bodies, but an elegant design beneath attached to the skeletal structure. The horses walked in unison and obeyed Gam Gam's silent commands because they were not alive. Mina watched their skeletal movements, and her eyes lit up. "Whoa."

Another chuckle came from Gam Gam, and Mina looked over. The necromancer watched her carefully, a small smile on her face. "You remind me so much of Asher, my grandson, whenever he learned something new. It's nice to see that excitement fill your face."

"Will we see your grandkids when we reach the cliff?"

Mina regretted the question as Gam Gam's face fell. Sadness filled her eyes, and her smile disappeared. Mina almost apologized when the necromancer said, "Yes, we will." She turned back to Mina, a forced smile settling on her face. "They passed away a year ago, in a terrible fire which claimed my daughter and her husband as well. It's why I became a necromancer. It's the only magic which can reach beyond the Veil of Death. It will be nice to see them again."

"I'm so sorry, Gam Gam." Mina's voice grew quiet as nerves took hold of her. She didn't want to say the wrong thing. She focused on Nugget instead and tried to make herself as small as possible.

"It's all right, dear." Gam Gam patted Mina's knee in a peace offering, her smile returning to some of its normal glow. "We all have our own tragedies. Poor Gibblet here is unable to wear any of my scarves!" Mina's own grin peeked out then.

Sir Gibblet sighed and grasped at his heart, or where one would be if he were alive. "Such wonderfully soft garments, forever out of my reach. Some days it's too difficult to continue unliving. Perhaps I will find glorious garments in the life beyond."

Sir Gibblet's melodramatic flare sent Mina into a fit of laughter, washing the darkness within her away. Her impossible dream of happiness shone again for that small instant. But Gam Gam's next words dampened her short-lived cheer.

"For now, let's focus on this sergeant," Gam Gam said. "Do you know where he would be?"

"He'd probably still be in the village. That's where he was when..." Mina trailed off.

"That's as good a place to start as any. Where is this village?"

The road crested a hill, granting them a view beyond the forest whose border they had been following. *West.* Hundreds of houses huddled in the valley below. Traffic filled the roads as the sun reached high into the sky, and people clustered near the small market at the village's heart. Unable to put voice to words, Mina pointed.

The wagon slowed, and Gam Gam looked out at the sprawling village. "I think we'll want to stop and pick up a couple friends before we head in."

4

Overripe pumpkins littered the field beyond the woods. Mina stood at its edge, one arm wrapped around the trunk of a large oak tree, and her stomach churned like an angry beehive. She watched the small wooden house beyond the field. The roof was painted Mina's favorite shade of blue, that of the sky right before the cloak of night.

Though it had been less than twenty-four hours since she had last seen the house, it felt like several months. Gam Gam told Mina she didn't have to go. That a minion could go for both of them. But undead could only do so much, and this was her home. Mina had to tackle this herself.

Mina scanned the surrounding area, and with no signs of soldiers or guards, she ducked low and ran from pumpkin to pumpkin. The round gourds weren't large enough to conceal her, but she hoped they would mask her presence enough to avoid alerting any passersby. Crouching low set the tired muscles in her legs flaring, and by the time she reached the house, they ached something fierce.

She paused at the oaken back door. It was sturdy enough to stand up to the wide range of weather and animals nearby. Her papa had greased the hinges not long ago, before the cold could settle in and make the job more difficult. She had opened the door hundreds of times before; a turn of the knob and a light push would do the job. But in that moment, it was the most difficult task Mina had ever faced.

She reached out with shaking hands, sweat greasing her palms as she twisted the handle. It turned on the second try and opened with an ease that went against Mina's expectations. It should have stuck. It should have been a battle. But it swung open as easily as every other time she had run in from caring for the pumpkins with her father. She had no choice but to look within. To see the empty corridor lit by the low sun peaking over the treetops behind her.

Her breath released and turned into a sob. There was nothing there. The body had been removed. Gam Gam had mentioned it would be, but a part of Mina hadn't believed.

The blood remained, tainting the floorboards a sickly brown. Mina kept her eyes averted, and her tears blurred the edges of her vision as she stepped around the worst of it. She was in her home again, and it felt anything but. It was familiar, and in the familiarity, there was comfort. But it was also hollow, a shell of what it should be. Without Papa, the heart and soul of the house was gone, dying when he did.

Mina wiped her eyes again and let out a breath. She had to get in and out before it was too late. She continued through the house as though in a dream, memories popping up everywhere she looked. The kitchen table where she would help her father gut pumpkins before baking their seeds into little treats. The padded rocking chair where her father would read her stories as she lay on the floor and dreamed them in her head. Sometimes she dreamed them outside her head too, though Papa would scold her when that happened and run her through the breathing exercises again.

Numbness seeped in past the welling emotions, filling her. She turned into the main hallway and stopped at the farthest door on the left. She pushed it open, revealing a familiar room. Not as familiar as her own, but one she'd been in many times before. She had curled up on that bed during thunderstorms, her father holding her until she slept. She had sat in front of that vanity trying on the jewelry and makeup that once belonged to her mother. Papa had laughed so hard when she came out with rouge caked on her cheeks and jewels lining her wrists, fingers, neck, and ears.

Now she sat in the same chair and watched her reflection in the dull mirror. Her hair fell to her shoulders in a tangled mess, and dirt patterned her face like a perverted distortion of the makeup from so long ago. She drowned in the oversized cloak, its hood drooping in front of her eyes and forcing her to push it back. She appeared even smaller than the last time she sat here.

Her hand ran across the jewelry containers and stopped at a small, red box. The outside was made of painted wood, the inside cushioned with a seam to hold two rings, each embedded with deep blue topaz gems and connected by a single cord. Her parents' wedding rings sparkled in the sunlight. Mina pulled them from the box and held them to her heart. Tears escaped her and raced down her cheeks. Was it possible to ever run out of tears? She couldn't possibly have many more before she would start shriveling up. Mina slipped the cord over her head but held the rings close as she sniffed and wiped her eyes.

She looked at herself in the mirror and smiled at her reflection and the two rings hanging around her neck—and then her heart stopped, and she whirled to face the man in the reflection. He was as silent as a hunter, not a noise made to announce his presence. She gaped silently as words disappeared, and her throat locked up.

"Pretty stupid to return here, girl." His voice was deep, his tone harsh and mocking. He was tall and bore a messy beard divided by a white scar down his right cheek and jawline. His eyes, a muddy green, were wide with excitement. The scarred man wore the leathers of a soldier and held a drawn knife. Mina had no doubt as to why he was here. "My luck that you'd fall back on sentimentality rather than do the smart thing and keep running."

Mina forced a breath, then another. Her nerves jittered, but her brain overcame the initial panic. She would be okay.

Gam Gam promised. "Pretty stupid to think I came alone," she said. She tried to sound confident, but her voice came out shaky.

He frowned, then his eyes went wide as two pairs of arms grabbed him. One hand twisted Mister Scar's wrist, and the knife clattered to the ground as he yelled. Then they dragged him, kicking and screaming, down the hall.

The capture happened too fast for Mina to react, and she almost missed the flash of gray, exposed bone. She raced down the hallway herself and arrived in time to watch as two undead, decked out in beautifully knitted scarves and hats, slammed Mister Scar to the ground in the center of the sitting room.

One of the undead was a zombie, as Gam Gam had told her. Flakes of rotten skin and tissue drifted off him as he moved, a scarf of blended greens complimenting his pallid skin. As he brushed against a chair, part of his forearm sloughed off—and not for the first time. Mina had named him Sloughy.

The other was considered an animated skeleton. There wasn't much difference between the two when it came to function, though maybe that was more advanced necromancy than Mina knew. The obvious difference was the severe lack of any flesh or organs. Instead, it was, as the name implied, a bunch of bones stuck together and capable of movement. The bones were pale gray with aged spots of brown, and the eye sockets were each an eerie, black abyss.

Around his neck dangled Gam Gam's latest scarf with a matching hat pulled snuggly above those empty eyes. For no discernible reason, Mina had named him Gerald.

Sloughy sat hard on Mister Scar's chest, knocking the wind from his lungs. Gerald had grabbed the man's arms and held them tight to the ground with surprising force, given the lack of muscle. Gam Gam and Sir Gibblet entered the house a moment later as Mister Scar gasped for air. When he tried to yell, Sloughy slapped a rotten hand across the man's mouth. Mister Scar's skin paled into a shade of sickly green as he went still.

"An excellent catch, Lady Mina!" Sir Gibblet said as he hovered nearby. "He will surely provide us with a boon of information."

"How are you doing, dear?" Gam Gam rubbed a hand along Mina's back, and Mina flashed a tiny grin.

"I'm fine," Mina lied.

"Shall I begin, my lady?" Gibblet asked as he drew his sword.

"Whatever it is you want, you're not getting it—blergh." The man choked on the zombie's hand once more, his face turning a darker shade of green. Mina felt bile rise at the back of her throat as well.

"You may begin," Gam Gam said. To Mina, she added, "Would you like to wait outside?"

"No." This man was a tie to Mikyal. Her hand drifted to the rings dangling just beside her heart.

"You vile creature, to invade the home of a small girl." Gibblet swung his sword in an arc, the air seeming to ripple around it. "You will answer our questions or face my wrath." He placed the point of the sword against the man's neck, just below the ear, and leaned down. "Tell me, have you ever had your soul rent in two?"

Mina shivered from the threat, but her eyes remained on Mister Scar. He went paler still and stumbled over his words. "Wh-what do y-you want?" He swallowed, coughed, and then spit out something that looked suspiciously like rotten skin. Then he gagged. Mina noticed some skin missing from Sloughy's finger and chose to believe it had always been missing.

"Do you work for Sergeant Mikyal?" Gibblet asked. When Mister Scar refused to answer, a zombie finger held below his nose proved a powerful motivator.

"Yes!" He took in large, gasping breaths when the finger moved away.

"Where does your master hide?"

"I cannot betray him. No matter what threats you throw at me, he will do worse!" The soldier was true to his word, taking the brunt of Sloughy's finger in silence.

"If you will not speak, then my blade you shall face." Gibblet raised his sword in the air, and the intruder quaked but remained silent, eyes clenched shut. "Shame," Gibblet said, and he brought the sword down, swiping through Mister Scar.

Mina was told what to expect, but it still felt anticlimactic. The man opened his eyes slowly, wincing as though he expected to see blood, then looked around in confusion.

"I apologize, my lady, I've done what I could." Gibblet hung his head as he sheathed his sword.

"Drat," Gam Gam said, her mouth quirked in thought.

Mister Scar blinked. "Th-that's it?"

"I'm a ghost, fool, what did you expect?"

"I'm the fool?" the fool said. "You lot are all under arrest! Let me go!" He fought against the skeleton's grasp to no avail.

Mina's heart sank. They had planned to trick the intruder with fear, but his loyalty to Mikyal had won out. Gam Gam was deep in thought, but they hadn't come up with an alternative plan. None of them were experienced in torture and interrogation—nor were they willing to resort to such tactics.

Mina, though, had one idea. A cold sweat broke out at the thought. And yet... they had no other choice.

She approached the struggling man and knelt beside his head. He tried to spit at her, but the zombie's fingers were faster and found purchase within his mouth, and the man turned nearly as pale as Sir Gibblet.

"Mina! Be careful," Gam Gam said.

"It's okay, I have an idea." Mina placed a hand on the man's forehead. Contact wasn't necessary. She had been able to reach Gam Gam's mind when hiding in the wagon.

But she knew what she was looking for, and being this close improved the connection. She pulled the power within her and felt it pulse through her veins, a burning sensation filling her, setting her nerves tingling. She reached out with her power to sense his mind, and gasped as she nearly drowned in its presence. Apparently contact helped a considerable amount. She pushed her power into the red-hot well of anger, fear, and shame that was Mister Scar's mind.

She became what everyone had always feared from her kind. There was a reason neuromancers made great interrogators. She delved into his mind and sought the answers herself.

Headquarters.

It was a simple prompt, something she hoped would provide her with an answer. Instead, she was flooded with hundreds. Her powers had never been clearer, each distinct memory floating in front of her like petals on a pond. She stood at the edge, as they drifted toward her. As she stretched toward the memories, they reached at her in turn.

The memories drifted closer, and she saw images flash across them. She had never felt so powerful—or so overwhelmed. She touched a memory, and the images blossomed within her own mind. She experienced the memory as if living it. A blur and a thud. Her hand lifted and blocked a blow she didn't see, and then another. She sparred with a friend and fellow soldier. A young woman who wore a vest, leaving her arms bare. Her muscles flexed as she moved the training sword, and her biceps were larger than Mina's head. Mister Scar's head? A feeling of jealousy floated by, and Mina didn't know if it was hers or Mister Scar's.

Naturally, she had pushed the image outward as she had with the wagon, painting the walls with Mister Scar's experiences. As she pulled herself free, the image of the scene faded. For a moment, she thought the memory lost, beyond her reach to access again. There was more to learn at the corners of her vision that she didn't quite catch. She needed to see closer.

But Mina returned to the pond, and the memory waited for her. She pulled it within her, and her mind melded once more with Mister Scar's as the room disappeared around her. She felt the grain of the training sword in her hand. She felt the sweat soaking her body. Her lungs heaved, but in a careful, practiced way.

"Is that it?" Mina asked. "I thought you were going to hit me."

"I have to go easy," the woman said. "You're still limping from the last time you took my hit."

She was right. Mina's left leg hurt. Though she ignored it, the limp was visible to a trained eye and—

Snap. The noise was clear as day, but Mina felt it within her. Something broke, the force reverberating through her. She shuddered, and before she investigated further, the memory faded from her mind like smoke in the wind. She returned to herself and to the pond where so many memories awaited her touch, crowding around her. But the memory she had held was missing, its space taken up by a dozen others crowded together.

She needed to focus on what was more important. There were answers to be gathered. She touched the next memory at random and pulled it within her. As she did, another memory brushed up against her and followed. Then another.

She became Mister Scar. But she was also a different Mister Scar. She received orders, but she wanted to eat first. She was walking around the town, *her* town but *his* mission. In a rage, her boss chased someone down. No, he was giving orders, and she had to follow orders. But not while eating. That was "me time." No one bothered her during "me time."

Mina's head prickled. She was all three Mister Scars, and she was herself. But she couldn't follow them, and her mind became overloaded. Like reading a different book with each eye, she comprehended nothing and gained only a headache from the attempt. More and more memories flooded into her, and the snippets flashed by faster and faster.

Within her father's house, the room played a mosaic of memories, dozens of them painting the walls as Gam Gam and Sir Gibblet raced to follow each new experience.

She walked, and she ate. She trained, and she worked. She hated, and she laughed—a mean laugh. She felt jealousy and comfort. Annoyance and boredom. She entered a dozen buildings, any one of them the current location of Mikyal. She saw the sergeant, over and over. Her mind ached as she lived a dozen memories with a dozen murderers. She saw herself, followed herself into the house. The grim satisfaction within nauseated her.

More and more memories clogged her brain and attacked her senses. Her perception fractured further, and then she screamed.

She jerked away, but the memories clung to her like burs, and in her panic, she could not understand how to release them. They snapped from the man, one by one, and that reverberation filled Mina with a cold realization. Each memory faded from her, and then there was nothing.

Mister Scar's mind locked up, and Mina's consciousness flooded into herself once more. Her hand clenched against the soldier's forehead as he bucked and seized beneath the grips of the undead. Mina fell back gasping, a cold sweat coating her body. Mister Scar's eyes rolled back into his head, and he gurgled wordlessly, saliva spilling from his lips. There were shouts, but Mina could not hear them over her own scream.

She crawled away from the man as the undead turned him to the side. Gam Gam dropped to the ground, hands at the man's face and neck. Mina couldn't watch. She rushed from the room, away from the second death she had caused.

You killed him! You killed him! YOU KILLED HIM! YOU—

Mina's fingers dug into her ears to block out the noise, her eyes squeezed shut to block out the sights, and she ran from the house, bouncing off furniture and walls.

She slammed against the back door, pulled it out of her way, and rushed out into the pumpkin patch at a stumble. Her foot snagged on a vine, and she toppled forward, one hand out to stop her fall. The hand smashed through a pumpkin, and her body followed, destroying it completely. The pulp smeared over her, but she ignored it, pulling herself up and sprinting to the edge of the woods, to the oak tree whose arms warded away the skies as if to protect her.

She dropped against the tree, knees pulled to her chest as the dying foliage crumpled beneath her. The wind gusted, and the leaves fell in droves, the oak's great protection lessening as the sky began to poke through, and autumn stripped the tree of its canopy. Nothing could protect her. She was poison.

She wept, huddled beneath her favorite tree, her parents' rings clutched in her hands.

Not long after the tears ceased, Gam Gam approached, weaving through the pumpkins with Gerald at her side. Mina pretended not to notice. The skeleton helped Gam Gam to the ground beside Mina. The wind blew a flurry of leaves by, and Mina remembered the memories that were petals in a pond. She squeezed her eyes shut against the thoughts.

"I—" Mina choked on the word, and a fresh stream of hot tears blanketed her cheeks. Between her sobs, the words escaped. "I killed him. I felt his mind crumble beneath my touch, but I couldn't stop it. I felt it collapse because of what I did. He died because of me!"

"You killed no one, dear."

The sobs slowed, then stopped. Mina opened her eyes again and rubbed at them. Then she looked at Gam Gam. "Really?"

"He'll be just fine. A little light on his memories, but he was able to get up and walk out. Doesn't remember us or why he's here, so we figured it was best to let him go."

Mina's heart was torn between grief and relief. She cried again, unable to stop herself. "I'm sorry!"

"You have nothing to be sorry about, Mina." Gam Gam pulled Mina into an embrace and held her there. "You're learning your powers, extensive as they may be. You're going to make mistakes, and those mistakes will have consequences. The consequences here, today, are minor. It could have been worse, but it wasn't, because you were able to withdraw your power quickly enough. You may have caused his memory loss, but you also saved his life."

"It wouldn't need saving if it weren't for me." The words fell from Mina, though with little conviction. The fight had left her, and exhaustion sat in her stomach instead. But the words were still true: it was Mina's fault.

"Yes, but he could have told us what we needed when we first asked. Or, perhaps, if I were better, I could have summoned an army of skeletal rats to hunt through the town. Or maybe if—"

"That's not fair!" Mina looked up and glared at the old woman. "I was the one who did it. So it's my fault."

"You should never have been in that situation, dear. Your powers should be practiced under better circumstances so you can master them. A mistake happened today, but disaster was averted. That is still a success, and there is one thing we can still do."

"What's that?"

"Remember it, learn from it, and grow." Gam Gam brushed a lingering tear from Mina's cheek. The grandmotherly woman smiled and said, "We are human, and we are fallible. But as long as we promise to learn and grow, then we are as good as we can be."

"I'll try, Gam Gam." Mina rubbed at her nose with a sleeve, then added, "Thank you."

"You're welcome, dear." Gam Gam brushed Mina's hair from her face and sighed. "You have a big heart, just like Evelyn. When this mess with the sergeant is cleaned up, we'll find a way for you to control your powers."

"But how are we going to figure out where Mikyal is now? The memories went too fast, and because I removed them, we don't even know where to look."

"Don't underestimate Sir Gibblet's eyes. They never miss a detail, and there were a lot of details for him to catch. He's already out searching."

"What do we do now?"

"First, let's grab some of your clothes while we're here. Get you into something that fits." Gam Gam grunted as she stood with Gerald's help. "Then, we find a cemetery."

5

A black shroud fell over the land as the sun set. Clouds rolled through the sky with the rising wind, blotting out what little light the moon provided. Gam Gam stood in the center of the cemetery, her arms raised as she softly chanted, her words lost on the winds. A shiver ran down Mina's spine that had little to do with the cold bleeding into the night air. Her hair blew across her face, and when she brushed it aside, she saw Gam Gam looking at her.

"Remember dear," the necromancer yelled over the howling wind. "Inexperience does not always mean ineptitude." Then she turned to the skies, and when she spoke again, it was with the power to pierce the Veil of Death. Leaves that glided along the breeze now shook until they tore into pieces. The sky crackled with faint purple lightning, and the hairs on Mina's arms and neck prickled.

To souls from Beyond, hear my cry.
Return to life, to death deny.
Cross my tether to old domains.

Renewed to save she who remains.
I have cozy knitted garments as reward!

"Why does she need to chant? She didn't have to do nearly as much for Sloughy and Gerald," Mina asked the spectral knight floating beside her.

"For who?" Gibblet's fluffy brows dropped in confusion. Mina pointed to the two undead, still as statues by the wagon. "Oh! Those two are constructs. They can understand simple commands, but mostly they're unthinking. Gam Gam has to focus her power to control them. What she's raising now is something far greater. She is tethering souls to their original bodies, reaching across the barriers of life and death. They'll have more control and understanding than, uh, Sloughy over there. It won't be like living again, but it'll be close."

"That's incredible. How does it work?" Mina asked.

"Well, um, do you know how to knit?"

"No."

"Me neither. Gam Gam explained it to me once like this. You know how when you knit it's normal?"

"What?"

"And then a purl is sort of inverted?"

Mina stared at the elderly ghost and his wild hand gestures and regretted the question.

"Well, the tether is like a special connection across the Veil. Even if they can reach their bodies, it doesn't matter, since you can't manipulate things as a spirit. I should know, you saw my sword pass through that intruder without pause. For something like Gerald, Gam Gam, um, knits connections to the body. These connections she can channel her power through and control the body. But it only works for her. For the souls to be able to move the corpses, she needs to invert those connections. Like purling instead of knitting. Or so she says."

"That makes no sense, Sir Gibblet."

"I may have forgotten a few things…"

Mina stared at the necromancer as a faint glow emanated from the old woman. But Sir Gibblet's description distracted her in a different way. She fidgeted with her sleeves, now more appropriately fitted thanks to a change of clothes. "What's the beyond like?" Mina asked. *What is it like where Papa is now?*

"I wouldn't know," Sir Gibblet said.

"What? But you're—"

"Dead? Yes." Sir Gibblet stared off into the distance, his features darkening. "I never passed on, though. When I was killed, it was in the defense of those I loved. I thought I had failed, and in my failure, I thought they died as well. Anger bled into my spirit and anchored me here, to this world. I became a revenant, an evil spirit." Sir Gibblet's eyes focused on his necromancer, one hand combing through his beard. "She helped me, cleared the anger from my soul. I've done a lot of bad in my post-life, and I wanted to do something good instead. That's why I'm following her now, because I know Gam Gam is a force of good in this world. I will do what I can to protect her and help her change the world for the better. Until the Call becomes too much, anyway."

"Oh." Mina struggled to think of any other word. How were there so few of them to say?

But Sir Gibblet came to her rescue again. He smiled down at her, a big grin that lifted his heavy mustaches and showed his ghostly teeth. An incorporeal hand touched her shoulder, and she felt a strange warmth where it sat. "Gam Gam is very good at helping others. She'll help you as she did me."

The tempest spiraled into a cyclone, and the roar of the winds drowned out Mina's thanks. The time for conversation had passed, yet murmurs rode the currents of the wind and filled the cemetery with an eerie chatter. Like a thousand voices speaking a thousand words. Pinpricks of light formed along the edges of the cyclone and funneled themselves toward Gam Gam, standing at the epicenter of it all, unperturbed by the sudden shift in weather.

Mina held the hood of her new cloak tight in one hand to prevent the fabric from smacking against her in violent bursts. The other hand held the hem to avoid it being ripped from her. Unfortunately, this left her hair free to punish her as it wished. Through squinted eyes, she watched the lights double. Then double again. A soft purple glow filled the cemetery, the dark gray headstones distinct against the black backdrop of shadow. Then the souls, for Mina now knew that was what the lights must be, dove into the ground. Where they landed, light rippled out like a stone tossed into a pond. Dozens of souls plunged to join their bodies, until the entire cemetery seemed to quiver beneath their barrage. Just as Mina began to wonder if it would ever end, the last spirit crashed home to its grave, and the world fell dark once more.

The winds calmed, and Mina released her hood to rub at her eyes. The shift to darkness played tricks on Mina's vision, making her believe the ground billowed. Then the ground billowed through the soles of her boots—her actual boots, this time—and she knew it wasn't a trick. An earthquake struck, and the cemetery shuddered. Gravestones tipped, and a rumble filled the air. Mina stumbled against the cemetery's fence as the ground bucked.

The first corpse broke its way through the ground where Mina had stood a moment before. A pair of hands clawed through the dirt. Its upper body followed, and the dirt flowed between its bones like water from skin after a bath. The ground collapsed behind it in a rush to fill the undead's vacancy. The moonlight peaked through the clouds, and a beam landed on the fresh corpse as if the world itself wanted everyone to see the wonder of the walking dead. Shreds of clothing clung to the skeleton's bones. Gray scraps of leather dangled from it, and Mina wondered if it had once been skin, so thoroughly rotten as to be unrecognizable.

Again and again, the corpses rose, punching and scraping out from graves that had been their final homes. No two looked alike, from the barely dead to bones so decayed they cracked with each movement.

Mina's eyes tracked the progress of the bodies as the cemetery churned so completely as to resemble her father's pumpkin field before first planting. Her eyes halted at an unmarked grave with a corpse fresh enough that his skin was still dark with life. The grave had been so shallow, he pulled himself up with ease and stood beside the small ditch that had held him.

Mina's vision blurred beneath an onslaught of tears as the corpse turned and looked at her. The dark brown stain covered his shirt, but his wound no longer oozed, having long since congealed with the stilling of his heart. He walked on unsteady legs, wobbling as badly as Mina's own began to. But she ran nonetheless, and he shuffled toward her.

"Papa!" Mina yelled as she slammed into her risen father. He smelled of mud and blood and felt cold to the touch, but she held him tight and cried into his shirt. His arms moved slowly to encompass and embrace her.

Mina did not notice the winds settle to a calm breeze nor the clouds dissipate from the sky. Moonlight filled the ruined cemetery as she pulled away from her father, uncaring of the dirt smeared on her face and clothes. "I've missed you so much," she whispered, and his cold, stiff thumb ran along her cheek to dry her tears.

Around her, more than fifty undead shifted into an organizable mass. Gam Gam had procured a makeshift walking stick that had once been a branch and now made her way across the uneven ground toward Mina. Her face was pale, and sweat matted her hair and ran down her temples. The necromancer wiped at her face to clear the worst of it by the time she arrived.

"Oh dear," Gam Gam said as she looked around at the gathered corpses. "I didn't expect quite so many. But I am glad I chose the right place so you could return." She placed a hand on Papa's shoulder and smiled at him. His own face shifted in an attempt to smile back, though it never quite manifested.

"I can't believe you brought him back." Mina's words were breathless with wonder.

"He answered my call. I just helped out a bit." Gam Gam winked. "I'll hold him and the others for as long as I can, but it is a complicated and tiring spell, so I can't guarantee anything."

Can you bring him back fully? Mina thought. But the words stuck to her tongue, and the moment to ask passed in a flash.

"Follow me," Gam Gam told Papa. "I have something special for you."

Gam Gam shuffled back toward the wagon. Mina followed, her father in step beside her as she pushed the ache in her heart away. She couldn't dwell on that wish. She had to focus on the time spent with her father. And she had to deal with the sergeant. She would have time with Papa after. Maybe even all the time.

The army of undead organized itself behind Mina and the others and followed. Sloughy hopped down from the now open wagon with the necromancer's chair in hand. Meanwhile, Gerald pulled wooden crates to the edge of the wagon, which Sloughy—after setting the chair up—placed beside the seat. When Gam Gam reached the wagon, Gerald procured a small chest and set it on the wagon's step. The older woman opened it and pulled a sweater from within; streaks of blue within purple sparkled in the moonlight as she held it up to Mina and her father. Mina's gaze traced the complex twists of the stitches, which resolved into a mesmerizing pattern. It was a beautiful sweater.

"It was supposed to be a gift to my son-in-law, Wyatt. Before the…" Gam Gam's eyes darkened, and she sighed. "Well, it doesn't matter now. It should fit you well enough and cover up that wound for you." Gam Gam held the sweater out not to Papa, but instead to Mina. She answered the unspoken question in a soft, sad voice. "He'll need help getting it on, dear."

"Okay." Mina reached for the sweater, her eyes locked on the sparkling fabric. She bit on her lip to hold back tears. She had at least a few moments with her father. They wouldn't be perfect, but she refused to waste them whining. "Come on, Papa, we'll get this on you."

Gam Gam settled into her seat, a crate of knitted attire to one side, as Mina led her father to a stump where he stood patiently, arms raised, while Mina worked the sweater onto him. It stuck against his arms and head as she tugged, and Mina tipped from the stump, spilling them both to the ground. A fit of giggles erupted from her, a happiness and comfort she'd never thought to feel again. When she saved her father from the sweater's tangled grasp, his head popped through the neck's hole, and a smoother smile clung to his lips. Her heart pulsed slower, her breath came easier, and some dark part of her mind brightened. Though he was unable to speak, Mina knew him well enough to understand.

"I love you too, Papa." They stood, and Mina tugged at the edges of the sweater, smoothing it out and pulling a few leaves free. He held his arms out in a questioning gesture that was so familiar she burst into laughter again. "It looks wonderful." She patted off a few more dirty spots on the sweater and gave a nod of success.

Father and daughter turned back to the necromancer and her train of undead. Mina frowned at the lack of progress. One by one, each undead approached Gam Gam and dithered over a hat, a scarf, or a pair of socks. When they chose, Gam Gam assisted in dressing them, then they gathered in a nearby clearing. The process was sure to take hours! Mina wanted to deal with Mikyal right away so she could spend more time with her father. Preferably somewhere that wasn't a cemetery.

Mina approached the necromancer, her father trailing, and watched the latest zombie stare at the three goods. When it chose socks, Gam Gam instructed it to lift a foot, then tugged the sock into place.

"Is this necessary, Gam Gam? Can they even feel the cold?" Mina asked.

"Of course it's necessary, sweetie," Gam Gam said as she pulled the second sock onto the zombie's other foot. "Just because they're undead doesn't mean they have to be neglected."

Mina paced as the line crawled past Gam Gam. The entire process put her nerves on edge, and there was nothing for her to do. The glossy eyes of her father tracked her. Sir Gibblet floated up next to her, his ghostly legs joining her march.

"You should try to rest, young mistress," he said. "You'll wear yourself out before the battle has even begun."

"Battle?" Mina froze in her pacing and stared at Sir Gibblet. "What battle? I thought we were just going to confront Mikyal and leave! There's going to be a battle?"

"Mikyal is inside of an inn with many of his troops. Gam Gam raised these undead to help us get to the sergeant." Sir Gibblet coughed into his hand as he looked around sheepishly. "It'll probably be more a skirmish than a battle."

Mina threw her hands up. "I'm twelve, Sir Gibblet. How am I supposed to relax before I enter a battle? Or a skirmish? Or a *whatever*? I didn't even know we were going to fight anyone. I've never fought before. I can't do anything."

"You aren't supposed to do anything," he explained. "You and Gam Gam will be apart from any fighting. Your father and the, uh…" His eyes glanced over to the undead helping Gam Gam. "*Sloughy* and *Gerald* will act as guards. There is no need to worry about the battle reaching you." He looked to Mina's father and added, "Or your father."

"Are you sure? What if something goes wrong?" She couldn't lose her father again. Even if he wouldn't be involved in the fighting, something could still happen.

"Then we will retreat and regroup with a new plan, but I have scouted the inn these ruffians are staying at and have deemed our numbers more than sufficient. The numbers of war are something I'm rather good at." He winked at her.

Mina looked between her father and the lengthy queue. Then she sighed. She could not change Gam Gam's plan, but there was one way to speed things up. Or to keep herself busy at the very least.

She walked up to Gam Gam, head held high. "Gam Gam," she announced.

"Yes, dear?" the wearied necromancer asked, wiping more sweat from her brow.

"These kind folk have returned to help me. It seems only fair that I should assist. Can I hand out some of your knitted things too?"

Gam Gam's smile brightened Mina's heart. "Of course, dear." Then she signaled to Gerald, who carried an empty crate over, which was then filled with a variety of knitted garments. "Remember to let them choose which kind they want. It's meant to be a reward."

"All right, Gam Gam," Mina said as she took the crate from Gerald. It was heavier than she thought, and she grunted as the weight transferred to her. She carried it to the stump and set it in front of her as she plopped down. Gam Gam communicated to the undead in a way Mina hadn't noticed, and twenty or so wandered over to her and formed a new line. Her father stood by her side. His smile formed more easily with each new attempt.

For a time, Mina silently proffered the choice of socks, hat, or scarf. She hated helping with the socks most; rotting did not improve the smell of feet. She reminded herself it was the least she could do for the souls willing to cross the Veil of Death to help her.

Mina began conversing to occupy her mind, and though her father wasn't able to reciprocate, he appeared invested in everything she talked about. She told him of how she found Gam Gam and how the necromancer helped her escape Mikyal's men once already. She told him of using her powers to trick the soldiers searching Gam Gam's wagon, and he frowned at her. But she assured him Gam Gam would still help her, and no one else knew. She did not mention the second use of her powers, the memory of Mister Scar's crumbling mind still an ache in Mina's chest. Finally, she told him of her plans for after. After the battle. After Mikyal.

"We're going to the coast," Mina said as a skeleton requested a beautiful, red scarf. Mina climbed onto the stump and wrapped it around the undead's neck, then it walked off to join the swelling ranks of clothed undead. "Gam Gam says it's beautiful there, and the water never ends. Well, I guess it does, but it doesn't look like it. No, you choose from these three." This said to the latest zombie, a younger woman who has been deceased a while given the state of her skin and who pointed past the offerings at something deeper in the box. "If everyone got to choose color too, we'd be here forever."

"Urrrrr," the undead woman growled and pointed again. Mina sighed and pulled out the yellow hat and held it up. The zombie nodded, something close to a smile creeping onto her lips, sending shivers down Mina's spine. She pulled the hat down on top of long, stringy strands of hair and tugged it snug. Then the zombie wandered off to join the others.

The next undead in line pointed into the crate past the offered goods, and Mina sighed again.

"Anyway," Mina continued as she searched the crate for the undead's requested item. "She said she became a necromancer to resurrect her grandkids, so we'll be doing that as well. Maybe I can get her to resurrect you too. You can come with us." Mina smiled up at her father whose face did not shift. He just stared back, Mina's heart dropped into her stomach until, with great effort, his lips raised at the edges. This time his smile was almost familiar.

At last, Mina pulled a hat of blended greens down atop the last of the undead, a skeleton whose fleshless grin somehow grew upon receiving the gift. Gam Gam had finished her group as well and patted her hands together. Gerald collected Mina's crate while Sloughy put away Gam Gam's supplies. Much to Mina's surprise, neither crate of offerings had run out. How many items had Gam Gam knitted? The supply seemed endless.

As Gam Gam circled around the wagon, she stumbled, catching herself against the wheel. Mina ran to her side, ready to support her. "Are you all right, Gam Gam?" She heard the panic in her own voice and tried to lower it from the screech it currently registered at. "You should sit down."

"I'm fine." Gam Gam waved Mina off. Her breath came in rapid gasps, like Mina's after a lap around the pumpkin patch while her father timed her to see if she could beat her previous record. But Gam Gam smiled at Mina as her breathing returned to normal. "Just a little tired, dear. It's more work than it looks is all. Nothing for you to worry about. Come on, let's get the horses ready."

"The horses?" Mina asked, but Gam Gam had already moved to unhitch Sebastian and Nora from the carriage. Mina followed, and the two of them worked to detach Sebastian's harness, with Gam Gam instructing Mina how to work the straps. Then the necromancer led him away from the cart.

"We want to make a bit of a spectacle, so we're taken seriously," she said, then with a wink, reached *into* the horse. Well, "into" was relative to who was watching, but Mina could see past the illusion, and she saw the necromancer pull a gem from between the horse's ribs. When it was free, the horse's true form showed. "What better way to do that than two ladies riding in on skeletal horses?"

Mina looked into the abyssal pits of Sebastian's eyes and figured Gam Gam had a point. They moved to Nora next, detaching her from the harness and removing a gem once more. The two undead horses stood sentinel in the moonlight, the glow off their exposed bones sending tremors through Mina. Sloughy and Gerald returned, each with a saddle. Seamlessly, they settled the tack onto the horses, fitting the saddles onto the much thinner frames of the de-fleshed horses than what they were designed for.

Then something seemed to click. Gam Gam's words registered through Mina's exhausted brain, and the panic set in once more. A cold sweat broke out beneath her clothes.

"Wait, I'm supposed to ride the horse? I don't know how to ride!"

"Don't worry, dear, you don't need to," Gam Gam said. "I'll control them the whole way and make it as easy as I can. Just hang on to that bit in the front, and you should be fine."

The undead army gathered around them, and some part of Mina thought they were adorable in their knitted gear. Then a zombie's face slid off his skull, and she chose to focus on those already lacking flesh.

As Sloughy and Gerald finished their work, a pair of undead helped Gam Gam into Nora's saddle. Mina stuck her foot in Sebastian's and tried to get up herself and fell backwards. Her father's hands clasped around her to steady her, then he boosted Mina into the saddle. A strange feeling swelled inside of her. From atop the fearsome horse she felt... powerful? Confident? She didn't know, but for the first time since returning home, her nerves seemed to settle, and she felt like she had a measure of control. She was ready to face Mikyal. Mina looked to Gam Gam, who smiled, then to her father, and he smiled in his own way. Sir Gibblet floated up between them, a determined grin on his face.

The end to all her pain and fear was half a town away. She would be free from Mikyal's hunt, and maybe she would even get her father back. If Gam Gam could save him too.

The necromancer made a show of snapping her reins flamboyantly, though Mina was sure it did nothing, and yelled out "Onward!" The horses walked forward. Sir Gibblet, Sloughy, and Gerald kept pace between them, and Mina's father hung by her side. Behind them, four columns of cozy undead marched in unison. Together, they ate up the ground between them and Mikyal and his soldiers.

6

The undead militia marched through the streets. The clacking of bones on cobbles rang through the still night like a hundred tossed dice. The few who roamed at the late hour sought side alleys or buildings to avoid the oncoming company, clearing the roads at the approach. Light from the homes bled into the street in spurts, blocked only by the various faces peering from the windows, which slunk away a shade paler as the army passed.

Mina sympathized with the frightened innocents and wished she could reassure them that all would be fine. However, there was no time to stop and explain that this undead army was a nice one. She could only hope no one would take it out on Gam Gam later.

Their destination was made evident by the two guards posted outside, both of whom spent more time than they ought to staring at the approaching army, jaws slackened. Their hesitance provided an opening for a few undead to sneak up from an adjacent alley. Two tackled the guards to the ground, and two more covered their mouths while a fifth pried weapons away. A quick and silent attack to avoid the attention of those within the inn. Mina hadn't even noticed the five undead leave their company. She glanced at Gam Gam, but the old necromancer was entirely focused on the guards.

The small band hauled the two guards out of sight while the main company split off to either side of the inn, huddling around windows and doors. Gam Gam stopped their horses right in front of the large double doors, an additional dozen or so undead grouped around them. The silence rippled across the undead as each came to a halt. The faint sounds of the inn's raucous crowd bled into that strange new stillness. Almost forgotten in the ceaseless clattering of the living dead, Gam Gam's heavy breathing became obvious once more. Her eyes were closed in concentration, then in a small whisper, without looking, she said, "Are you ready?"

Mina's nerves renewed in force, her palms grew sweaty around the saddle's pommel, and a new worry of slipping from the saddle filled her. She dried her hands on her trousers, though it didn't help much. She exhaled and focused. She had faced more difficult things than this. She had run all night through the woods. Barefoot! She had faced down soldiers with her magic. She had crept into the house where her father died. Her nerve would not vanish here. She looked to Sir Gibblet, who nodded and flashed her a big grin. She looked to her father, who placed his hand on her thigh, the soft pressure radiating calm through her body. She was ready to end this.

"Yes," she said, and she stood tall in her saddle, determined to face whatever she needed to.

"Hold on tight," Gam Gam said.

"Wha—?" The unfinished word lingered as the horses reared up in unison and stepped forward on their hind legs. Mina's confidence evaporated, and she clung to the saddle. Her eyes bulged, and her legs clenched against Sebastian's sides. Then his hooves (Did he still have hooves? Mina wasn't sure but didn't want to check at that moment.) slammed into the front doors synchronously with Nora's. The doors slammed open with an earsplitting crash, and one flew off its hinges and slid across the common room floor.

Mina watched, crouched low over her saddle with her muscles locked tight, as the men and women jumped from their seats, their mugs clattering to the floor as they stared open-mouthed. Not one grabbed for weapons, clearly flummoxed by the intrusion of an old woman and a young girl on skeletal horses. The soldiers' hesitance once more tipped the battle (or skirmish, or *whatever*) in favor of the undead, and it would never tip back.

"Remember to subdue only. No killing," Gam Gam said, then the hells broke loose in the inn's common room. Every window shattered at once as undead flung themselves through the panes of glass and smashed through the side doors. Those nearest Mina and Gam Gam flooded past through the main doors. Screams emanated from beyond the doors where Mina guessed the kitchens might be. The bartender ducked behind his bar, a large bottle in hand as he did so. A woman in an apron dove under a table, smacking it hard enough to send a few more pewter mugs rattling to the ground. The soldiers grabbed for weapons at last, but few had them out before the swarm of corpses reached them.

The undead moved like a wave, pulsing in through every opening and crashing over everything and everyone. The sounds of wood breaking and people screaming echoed out into the night. One woman utilized a table knife to stab at a skeleton only to have the blade catch within its ribs. Another man used a chair as a weapon, and though he did knock the head off of one zombie, three more tackled him to the ground. Sir Gibblet flew around the room in a frenzy as he yelled orders to the undead and acted as a distraction to the living. He swooped down toward one soldier, spectral sword shimmering in the air, and as she recoiled from his attack, two skeletons took the opening to drive her to the ground. The smell of mud and spilled beer wafted up to Mina as her gaze darted around the room, trying to take it all in.

One zombie pulled the bartender from behind the bar as he hollered out a surrender. It pulled him to an isolated area, safely away from the bulk of the brawl, and sat on his chest to hold him still. Then the undead held up a bottle and offered it to the bartender. The man accepted greedily, the awkward position causing more liquor to spill from his mouth than to be swallowed.

On the other side of the room, in the thick of the brawl, one large man swung a warhammer around at wary undead whenever they approached. He had already crushed two and looked eager for more victims, but then six undead charged. Two from the front, sacrificed to the hammer's blows, and four from behind. They wrestled him to the ground, all four working to hold his limbs still and pry the weapon free.

One man raced across the common room, dodging around grasping hands until a skeleton slammed into him, and the two crashed through a table. The man kicked the animated bones away and sat up as blood squirted from his nose and down the front of his shirt. He blanched as he took in the gush of crimson. Over the racket of battle, Mina heard the man as he said, "Oh no, Krystle hates it when this happens." Then he fainted.

Shouts echoed from the kitchen doors as a plump man in an apron rushed out, frying pan in one hand and a skeleton on his back. He bucked like a feral horse and swung the frying pan above his head, trying to rid himself of his assailant. It never quite connected with the undead's skull, and a zombie used the distraction to crawl in front of the cook's legs. The cook toppled into a table and launched a glass of ale across the room. It collided with a soldier's head, and a one-armed skeleton took the opportunity and jumped on the soldier just as the cook's own skeleton clambered atop him.

The doors to the kitchen dangled loose, and Mina thought she saw a zombie, notable due to a missing scalp, walk by wearing an apron and holding a mixing spoon. But as she tried to focus on it, a roar resonated through the common room and she turned in time to watch as a woman hurled herself from the second floor banister, a zombie in her clutches, and crashed into a table, breaking it in half and drenching both of them in beer. The zombie's head rolled away from their body, eyes searching for someone to bite onto if nothing else. From the wreckage of the table, the woman rose. Her shirt had its sleeves torn free, for no sleeves could hold those arms. She was taller than most in the room and, more likely than not, stronger. Mina recognized her from Mister Scar's memories, and she eyed the biceps with a hint of jealousy–hers or a remnant of Mister Scar's, Mina wasn't sure. For a moment, she wondered what it would take to become as muscular, then she shook her head and returned her focus to where it should be.

Bicep Woman staggered from the table, woozy from the fall, and five undead took advantage and struck together. Even then it was a close call as the small mob bounced from wall to bar in a struggle. One zombie lost an arm, and a skeleton was beaten to pieces with the same severed limb.

But, eventually, they staggered the giant woman, and with one undead stationed at each limb, they were able to hold her down even as she continued to roar and twist beneath them.

As suddenly as it began, a calm fell over the common room. Bicep Woman, recognizing the loss, ceased her howling. That appeared to signal the end as the others stopped their shouts and struggles too. The soldiers looked a mixture of bored and frustrated, now knowing that death was not likely to occur. The inn's employees looked bewildered and frightened, though the undead sought to make them comfortable. The cook was even eating a snack, though Mina had no idea where he had retrieved it from. The battle was over, a resounding victory for the necromancer and her army of undead.

Mina looked over the risen, most seated on soldiers as if they were furniture. Her gaze came to rest on those that were destroyed, and a pang of guilt and loss stabbed through her. The one Bicep Woman drove into the table clung to her boot with its rotten teeth. But most of the others were unmoving, their eyes stilled. They had crossed the Veil of Death to help her today, and though they would have returned eventually, she was still sad to see them leave by someone else's actions rather than their own choice.

Mina heard a grunt and turned to see Gam Gam dropping to the ground with Sloughy and Gerald to either side. She looked down and noticed Papa's hand in hers; his cold, bloated fingers were almost life-like as they warmed under her grip. Again she thought of him back, resurrected fully, and how wonderful it would be. For now, she had to make do.

Mina swung her leg over the saddle and dropped into her father's waiting arms. He set her gently on the ground, and the two of them joined Gam Gam at the entrance. Something brushed against Mina's leg, and she flinched away with a yelp. Papa jumped in front of her, and Gam Gam wobbled in response. Nugget, far from where he should be, wandered past and plopped down on the cook's stomach and curled into a ball. He looked to all the world as if he were now taking a nap. The bewildered cook pet the skeletal cat with his free hand, each stroke more sure than the previous.

"Foolish cat," Gam Gam muttered and entered the common room.

Mina wondered if there was something different with Nugget. He didn't seem to act like any other undead Gam Gam had risen except maybe the soul-tethered. But before Mina could ask, Sir Gibblet swooped down from the second floor and landed in front of Gam Gam. "The area is cleared. The rooms are empty or barricaded on the second floor. I've instructed a few of the undead to continue on to the third with the same instructions."

"Good," Gam Gam said. "Did you find the sergeant?"

"I believe he is in the far room on the third floor."

"Miky?"

Gam Gam and Sir Gibblet looked down at Bicep Woman who gazed up at them with a half-lidded, bored expression.

"It is Sergeant Mikyal we are looking for," Gam Gam said.

"Yeah, he's in that room. Sculpting, most likely," Bicep Woman said.

"The man I saw was indeed sculpting," Sir Gibblet added.

"Then we've found who we're here for." Raising her voice to the undead in the room, Gam Gam added, "Those who are not busy restraining these fine folk, please form up on me."

"Good luck," Bicep Woman mumbled. Gam Gam did not appear to hear, but Mina did, and those words worried her. Why wasn't the woman more worried for her sergeant?

The unoccupied undead left their companions to form up near Gam Gam. A zombie, her face askew like a poorly-fitted mask, came from the kitchens carrying a large pot barehanded. Steam rose from the concoction within, and smoke trailed from the zombie's hands. Mina grimaced at the faint sounds of sizzling she suspected came from the hands rather than the food, though her mind could have been playing tricks on her. She looked away, seeing the bodiless head clinging to Bicep Woman's boot, and a realization struck her. Maybe the undead were unable to feel pain. Sir Gibblet said the spirits puppet the bodies, but if not all the connections are present, pain was as likely as any to be severed. Maybe more likely since most necromancers liked to use the undead as weapons.

The unliving cook set the hot pot of stew beside the living cook and fed him a spoonful. He nodded in agreement, and the zombie woman smiled and wiped her blackened hands on her apron. Then she left the stew to cool there and joined the others, only numbering a half dozen, to continue upstairs.

"Wait!" Bicep Woman yelled out as the necromancer gathered her risen, and Sir Gibblet ordered them into formation.

"Yes, dear?" Gam Gam asked. Mina was surprised to hear such kindness being directed at someone who was supposed to be the enemy.

"Is this all you? All these undead?"

Gam Gam turned, a proud, sincere smile forming on her lips. "Why, yes, it is. Not so bad for an amateur. Don't you think, Mina?"

Mina smiled back. "You're the best necromancer I have ever seen."

Sir Gibblet took the lead, their incorporeal scout, and the remaining undead took their positions. Four to the front, followed by Papa and Mina. Then Gam Gam, Sloughy, and Gerald with the rear taken up by the remaining two soul-tethered. They climbed to the second floor, and Mina's initial jubilation crumbled as Gam Gam struggled with the steps. Her breathing grew heavier, her face paler. They had to wait on the second floor for Gam Gam to regain some stamina while Sir Gibblet scouted ahead to ensure those he sent on had completed their tasks. Mina offered assistance, but the necromancer waved her off and said it was nothing.

When they resumed their progress, a deep worry blossomed in Mina. All her anxiety flooded back into its familiar locations, and her chest burned with the pain of it. They had made it this far, it couldn't go wrong now. Just a little longer and they would all be fine. They had to be fine.

When they arrived at the door to Mikyal's room, Mina's retinue was down to six. Gam Gam's additional recruits had branched off to deal with trouble along the way, leaving Papa, Sir Gibblet, Sloughy, and Gerald representing the undead. Gam Gam and Mina remained as the only two still with a pulse. Gam Gam slowed with each step, and exhaustion began to hammer at Mina as well. It was as if all her fear and panic and hope had turned into loops of Gam Gam's yarn around her shoulders. Unnoticeable at first, but each new skein adding more weight until she felt as though she would collapse beneath it all. But she refused to give in, not while Gam Gam continued on.

Gam Gam opened the doors, and they stormed the room with the confidence of a victorious army—that being shaky, nervous, and surprised to have made it this far. Mikyal stooped over a desk, thick spectacles perched atop a beak of a nose and short, pointed mustaches on his upper lip. He wore a tan apron covered in smears of clay and held a scalpel in one hand, which he used to cut into a lump of wet clay on his desk. His steady hands continued with surgical precision despite the distraction. His eyes—irises the dark black of a bottomless pit and radiating the same unnerving energy as one—never left the clay project in front of him.

This room had been modified from the others. For one, several rows of shelving had been hammered into the walls around the entire room, even above the bed. Not a section of wall was wasted, and not a section of shelf went unused in turn. Strange clay figures stood along the shelves, varying in height, the tallest being four feet and the smallest no more than six inches. Although they were vaguely humanoid, none would be mistaken as so with their exaggerated features. One had lengthened arms with massive hands, while another had an enormous mouth and rows of sharp teeth. Mina's gaze ran along the figures as she wondered how long it must have taken to create them all. And why would he bring them with him?

"Oh good." Mikyal's voice snapped Mina's attention back to him. "Set the girl over there. You're dismissed." When no one moved or spoke—Mina wasn't the only one surprised at the clipped reaction towards his intruders—Mikyal continued. "One of my men will get you the reward if that is what you're waiting for." His eyes had left his project just long enough for that last sentence, then he returned his attention to his work, and his hand moved once more in small, careful twists of the wrist.

"I think you're mistaken," Gam Gam said. "I'm not here to do your bidding. I'm here to request you leave Mina alone. Her powers are not a tool for your personal gain."

Mina was glad for Gam Gam's presence. Her own mouth clenched shut as Mikyal's eyes slid from his project and stared at the newcomers. She wanted to scream, to push him out the open window, to do anything. But instead, she shook with fear beneath his gaze. The man who had upended her whole life, who had stolen her father from her, was right in front of her. And yet she still felt so powerless.

Mikyal set the scalpel down with the same exacting care in which he used it, then removed his glasses and placed them alongside the knife. "Is that so?" His voice held no fear or worry. He rose from his seat, straightening his humped back and unfurling his long limbs. When he stood, he was taller than anyone else in the room by more than a head. "I decline. I shall take the girl by force if necessary. Left to her own devices, her powers could destroy the minds of innocents." Mina flinched at the accusation, and Mikyal's eyes studied her as he added, "If she hasn't already."

Her eyes dropped away from the sergeant and studied her own feet. Her breathing turned rapid, and her calming techniques deserted her.

"Please reconsider," Gam Gam said between her own heavy breaths. Despite her fatigue, her voice still held authority. "Violence is no way to solve problems, and I am loath to continue with it. If it wasn't obvious, Sergeant

Mikyal, your forces have been subdued by my own. There is no one to come help you now."

"My forces?" Mikyal raised an eyebrow as his dark eyes studied her. A chill darkened the room and rose bumps across Mina's arms. "Those soldiers are merely pawns and servants, meant for no more than simple tasks." His arms spread to either direction, fingers extended, palms up. A spark of green flashed in the wells of his eyes, and Mina felt an unnatural thickening to the air. "*These* are my forces."

Rattling resounded from every direction at once. The clay figures shook and shifted, their eyes glowing a bright green as they came alive. Mina turned to the door and found it blocked by two taller figurines as the rest jumped from their shelves. Their movements were slow and jerky, and a hollow clank resonated with each step. Mina clung to her father's arm as the terrible clacking radiated from every direction and overwhelmed her. Sloughy and Gerald tried to take up protective positions around them, but they were only two undead and Mina couldn't see how they could stop so many. There were hundreds of figures surrounding them, forming one perfectly inescapable mob. Papa shifted to stand in front of Mina, his arm still clutched in her own.

"Golems." Gam Gam was nearly inaudible over the figures' incessant rattles. She looked so pale now. How long had she been that way? How long could she continue? She was wiping sweat from her face every few seconds now, and her eyelids drooped farther. "You're a vitamancer."

"Yes." There were no wasted words when the sergeant spoke. He held the confidence of someone who understood the situation. He knew the outcome already. They had only to reach its conclusion.

"We must change our tactics," Sir Gibblet said. His eyes darted erratically across the golems, then stopped at Mikyal. "Be prepared to push your way out of here. I shall do what I can to distract this disreputable sergeant." Gibblet readied his phantasmal blade. Before a word could be uttered, he charged over the heads of dozens of clay figures. Gam Gam's yell died on her lips.

"Now learn why I was once feared, Sergeant!" Sir Gibblet's words echoed with a rage and hatred Mina had never felt before, and that hate coalesced into a red tint that filled the room. His body warped, solidifying until it obscured the air. The edges of his form blurred into a mist, and his eyes burned red. "I have lived as a knight for thrice your age and then as a revenant for a hundred years more!" The air rippled around Sir Gibblet's blade as it arced toward Mikyal. "You are nothing—"

The blade stopped, the strike halted by Mikyal's hand, now encased in a strange glove of green energy.

"Your threats are meaningless, spirit. In the end, you are but death energy trapped on this world and nothing more. I shall end your suffering."

The ghostly knight yanked at his sword, but it failed to budge. Mikyal's free hand rushed up and tapped Sir Gibblet on the chest. Green light burst through the spirit, and he shredded apart like a popped bubble. Mina had expected a roaring noise to accompany the action, but there was only silence in its wake.

The golems had gone quiet, and in the absence of their constant rattling, Gam Gam's voice was clear. A single, whispered word, laced with horror.

"No."

Mina pulled closer to her father. Her body shook with fear. Energy pulsed up and down her arms and legs, preparing them to move. To fight or run. To do something. But there was nothing she could do, and now Sir Gibblet was gone because of that uselessness. Gone forever, a small part of her mind told her.

"You and I are alike, necromancer." Mikyal circled around his desk, the golems shifting to make a path. "Alike, but opposite. You embody death, have the ability to twist it to your will. Yet you fight against it. I can see it in your heart, the way you crave life. You dress up your constructs like they have needs. You treat them like humans when you should dominate them. You work against your necromancy, and it makes you weak. I have the strength you dream of. To create life." Mikyal's eyes scanned them once more and stopped on Papa. "You can bind the soul of my old friend to his corpse, but that does not mean Kelis is living. He will never be your father, girl, no matter how much you cower behind him."

Mina squeezed her father's arm tighter, panic rolling through her body. It is him. *It is!* She had seen how he reacted. The smiles he passed to her. His protectiveness.

Papa remained silent against the accusations.

"You underestimate me," Gam Gam said. "Just because I'm old—"

"It has nothing to do with your age." Mikyal's black eyes burned with annoyance as they snapped back to Gam Gam. "I don't underestimate anyone. What can you do against me? I am the embodiment of life. *True* life. Something you strive for with this falsity of yours. You cling to the old, the dead, the rotten. Any life you create will be a poor substitute. An abject failure. The real power of life is mine. The power to create it where there was none.

"You are exhausted. Your power is at its end, and it's taking everything you have to tether what few spirits you've raised. I have done what you wished you could. I have created an army, and you choose to face me with dolls in fancy knitting. You are a frail, old lady and a little girl. What can you *possibly* do against me?"

Mikyal waited for an answer, but Gam Gam stayed silent. Everything he said was true; there was no escape. Mina had led them into this pain. If she had been stronger, or if she had run away instead, then maybe...

Mikyal stepped closer until only Papa stood between her and the sergeant. Mina looked around her father, and a flash of metal shone green with the aura of the room. The knife appeared within Mikyal's hand as if by magic.

"I'd rather not have to stab you again, Kelis." Mikyal angled his blade at Papa. "Though, it will not bother me to do so. Let me have the girl, and I'll let you return to the afterlife in peace. She will be taken care of, under *my* mentorship. It is the least I can do for an old friend."

Mina felt ice flood her veins, and her vision blurred against the terror.

Papa shifted Mina out of the way again, a barrier between Mikyal and his goal for the second time in as many days, and Mina saw him as he had been, far more lively than now, standing in the pumpkin field, his gaze fixed on the soldiers approaching.

Mina screamed. It was incoherent and wordless. It was her pain, all of it, bundled into one final outburst. The pain of losing her father, and of losing him again. The pain of uselessness, of endless tears. The pain of Gam Gam's tireless aid and of letting her down in the end. It was the sound of the pain she wanted to be free from.

A flash of white whistled past Mina and slammed into Mikyal's face. His glare disappeared in an instant, replaced with surprise, shock, and agony as he staggered back and slammed into his desk. His clay project dropped to the floor in a splatter. Nugget clung to the sergeant's face, claws digging in and scraping across his right eye. Mikyal grasped the cat's spine and threw the bony creature against the wall into a crowd of golems. Blood ran down the side of his face, as he held a hand to his wounded eye.

"Seize the girl and kill the others!" Mikyal roared.

From the corner of Mina's vision, the streak of white hurtled up to the window frame. Nugget meowed silently to Gam Gam, then jumped into the night. How it evaded the now aggravated army, Mina was not sure, but the attention turned to them again, and the golems moved forward.

Gerald pushed against the surge. One of the golems swung its oversized fist into the skeleton's knee, snapping the bones loose and sending him clattering to the ground. One golem with a misshapen arm launched a second, smaller golem, no bigger than Mina's forearm. It flew straight at Sloughy and clutched onto the zombie's face as he was knocked back. Unable to get a solid grip on the rotten flesh, the golem slid from Sloughy, bringing much of the zombie's face with. Sloughy took the opportunity to kick the small golem and shatter it against the wall.

Papa took a step forward, ready to charge the sergeant. Mikyal lifted his knife in defense, but clay hands grasped Papa's arms and legs, bringing him to a halt. Gam Gam wobbled where she stood, her eyes glazed, then fell to the ground with a thump.

"No!" Mina pulled at the arms holding her papa in desperation. She looked at Gam Gam, and worry clenched her heart in its fist. "Stop! Please!" She turned back to Mikyal, the clay arms unmovable in her grasp. "Stop! Let them go, and I'll do whatever you say!"

"Mina..." Gam Gam's voice was barely more than a whisper. She sounded so tired, her breathing so labored now. Mina forced herself to look at Mikyal. The only person who had the power to stop what was happening.

Mikyal raised his hand, the one with the knife in it, and the golems' rattles stilled. Gerald flopped around on the ground near Gam Gam, pushing against the wave as best he could. Sloughy, nearer to Mina, was still standing, though did not seem to fare much better. Papa was in one piece, but those hands still held him tight.

Mikyal's gaze pierced her with the unbearable heat of anger. The first emotion Mina had seen him display. "I think not," he said, lowering his hand. The clattering began again, and despair crushed Mina as easily as the wave of golems would soon crush them all.

She fell to her knees as time fled from the room. The golems renewed their assault. Gerald lost another limb as Sloughy had his scarf ripped from him. The stub of Gerald's mostly missing arm came up to knock away a golem even as another slipped through the inadequate guard and hurtled toward Gam Gam. The elderly necromancer raised her makeshift cane in time to bat it away, though the clay figure recovered quickly. The hands grasping Papa tightened and pulled as if to tear him apart in front of her.

And Mina watched. She had been so useless at every step. She was worse; she was a burden. She was the *reason* all of them were here. She killed her father, just as she told Gam Gam. And now she was going to kill him again, along with the kindly, old woman. It was all her fault.

Evelyn put too much on her shoulders just as you are doing now, Gam Gam's voice rang through her head, the memory barreling through her self-destructive thoughts. *The actions of others are never your fault.*

Mina watched the chaos of the room unfurl. The golem reached Gam Gam, and a few more tugged Sloughy to the ground. Papa fought against his captors, but they succeeded in pulling him to his knees. Clay hands tugged at her cloak, pulling her toward the wall and away from the others.

We're alike in that way, misunderstood and judged for what we can *do instead of what we* actually *do.*

No. Mina wasn't helpless. She wasn't useless. The jolt of her power flooded her veins and ran wild with her emotions. She escaped Mikyal's soldiers twice. Gam Gam raised an army to get her here. She couldn't let it end this way.

She slipped from her cloak, the buttons tearing off as she tugged against it, and ducked past the grasping arms of the golems. She stumbled into the open space between her papa and the sergeant and pulled herself to full height, her breathing rapid but controlled in the way of her exercises. Then she screamed, not with her pain, but with her love. With her desire to protect just as she was protected.

"NOOOOO!"

Her voice cracked as her anger flared. Tears burned hot in her eyes. *I have learned in my time that if two men are chasing a young girl, it is never the girl's fault.* It wasn't her fault; it was Mikyal's fault. Everything was *his* fault!

Her power exploded from within her in a rush and slammed into Mikyal with everything she could muster. Which turned out to be significantly more than Mikyal could defend against. His mind broke open at her touch, and he fell against the desk in shock.

Vitamancy! First, his magic.

She could see the white of his one eye, terror and anger flaring within. She could feel the hands of the clay figures on her wrists and shoulders. They tugged her to her knees in desperation to stop her, and she felt the collision with the floor.

But she also saw the pond within his mind, the petals that were his memories floating to the surface. Hundreds of them overlapped as she reached out for them. She tugged at them, and the memories flooded into her. She didn't parse through them, didn't try to watch them. She consumed them, and, as with Mister Scar, she tore the memories from Mikyal's mind as she would berries from a bush. The memories lasted only moments, but the sensations and images bombarded her nonetheless, overwhelming her with smells and tastes. With touch and emotion. All swirled together into a jumbled mess, and still she pulled more within.

Some part of her was aware of that visceral scream, of the wordless roar that belted from her lungs. But her mind was consumed by the living memories, the second life she lived at an expedited rate. The life of a vitamancer.

She licked at her lips. The taste of clay filled her mouth. The earthy texture brought her closer to the world and its great life source. The small ball of wet clay shifted beneath her hands as her long fingers smoothed grooves into it. She held a scalpel for the detail work, and a small tremor shook her hand as she held her breath and made the minuscule slices needed. It would live regardless, but the art was important. She—

—stood in front of three clay figures. Her fingers ran across the shells hardened by the kiln. She had painted each distinctly, adding minute details to bring their look alive. Then she brought their forms alive. Her body thrummed with the life magic, the taste of earth filling her mouth, and she pushed her magic into the clay figures. They shook with life, their limbs moving despite having been rock-hard a moment earlier. And that beautiful, green light flashed alive in their eyes. She could feel them in her mind; she could tell them what to do. She made them march on the table, then—

—the lesson began. She was younger, no more than ten, but it was hard to remember specifics. Her mentor scribbled on a chalkboard and talked about the concepts of life. The power we pull and harvest from the world tree, the great giver of life. We can be doctors, animators, or soldiers. The world was kind to vitamancers, the most important branch of magic. And she would be the greatest among them. Animation would be her branch. No one became famous for healing, and the best healers were sent to the Eternal Emperor. No, she would build her own army, one of golems, and she would be unstoppable. She could feel the clay in her hands already, taking shape into—

—more, and more, and more—

She sat through dozens of lessons. She trained as a vita-mancer and as a soldier. Her gift was strong, and so they catered to her. Helped her cultivate it into something great for the empire. She didn't care about the empire, but their desires aligned, and so she was happy.

Each memory that passed through her mind flashed alive in the room. Golems marched along the walls. The mentor and his incessant scribbling on the ceiling. His experiences carving and painting hundreds of clay figures. Every moment was scoured from Mikyal's brain, and he watched them fade before his eyes. Tears turned the right side of his face into a crimson river.

The flood of memories went, and when Mina's mind stilled, so did the golems. The green light in their eyes died one by one, and their movements grew stilted as they transformed back to the kiln-hardened clay figures they once were. The clattering, that *terrible* clattering, was no more.

Everything was still within the room but for the rapid rise and fall of three living chests.

Mina stood, and the arms restraining her shattered, earthen bodies tipping and fracturing into hundreds of pieces. A faint, orange plume of dust rose from their remains. The golems around the room shattered and disintegrated as Gam Gam and the undead pulled themselves free. The necromancer drew herself into a seated position, with a much more defleshed Sloughy at her side. Gerald searched for his missing bones to piece himself back together. Papa rose from a reddish-brown dust cloud, unharmed, and walked to her side.

Mina's eyes never left the crumpled, defeated sergeant who slumped against his desk. Tears ran steadily down his cheeks as he looked at his own hands. Droplets fell from her own chin, surprising her. She shouldn't be sad. He was awful and deserved the punishment. Yet, deserved or not, the punishment was cruel and twisted her stomach into knots. Her tears continued to drip from her chin.

Mikyal's memories had long since left her mind, but she knew it wasn't over. Mikyal the vitamancer was but one aspect of this man. He had desires, he had aspirations. And while he remembered Mina, he would hound her. While he remembered Gam Gam, she was in danger. He couldn't remember any of it.

Mina stepped forward, then staggered. A pair of undead hands caught and steadied her. Her legs were numb and weak, and they shook beneath her weight as if her brain wasn't sure how to move them. She pushed herself forward, Papa's arm a constant comfort around her.

"Mina," Gam Gam croaked. "He's beaten, we must leave." She leaned her head against Sloughy as though the act of holding it up was too much. "It's over."

"It's not over." Mina coughed, her throat scratchy with pain. She wanted to explain more, to warn Gam Gam. She had seen it inside the man. She had experienced what it was to be Sergeant Mikyal and knew that this man would never give up, never forget this. Not unless Mina made him.

She knelt on aching knees and placed a hand on Mikyal's face, the side that wasn't ruined. His gaze had been distant, distracted, but at her touch, he snapped back into the moment, and his attention returned fully to her. She saw the rage that burned within. Saw the shame and the anger. She had thought him so emotionless before, but now everything was so clear. Their tears mirrored each other as they stared. One with a gaze filled with hate and rage, the other with sadness and love.

A terrible snarl warped his face, and he growled at her. "You—"

"I'm sorry."

Mina.

Again, she sent her power crashing into the man's mind, and again the memories floated up to her. Easier than before. So she grabbed them, pulled them into herself, and broke them free. Every memory that was tied to her.

She saw recent ones, from the room they were in but inverted as if from a twisted mirror. She tore at those so Gam Gam would be freed from his wrath. She saw meetings with soldiers, tales of a thief to capture. She saw—

—her mother stood in front of her. Beautiful and young. Recognition flared, though Mina had never seen her before. Shame filled her. Shamira should have been hers, but then Kelis came along. She didn't deserve a weak man like that. The room they stood in was small, the sheets on the bed bloodied. Shamira was pale and sweating. The birth had already happened, that was clear. It would make things easier, at least.

"No need to do anything rash, Shamira," Mina said. "I know what you are, and I would never hurt you."

"Only imprison me?" Shamira said. "Use me to meddle with the minds of your prisoners and enemies? What is it you want from me, Mikyal? To steal secrets or just wipe the minds of those in your way?"

Pain stabbed into Mina's chest from beyond the memory. Some sense of her felt it, but the version of her who desired Shamira was unperturbed. "Give me the child, and you and your husband can live in peace." She looked around the small room, though there was not much to see. "Where is Kelis anyway? Hiding with the child?"

Shamira laughed. A single bark filled with grief. Fresh tears rolled down her cheeks. "Minerva died. She was stillborn. He has gone to bury our daughter, and you're here to try and steal her from us. I suppose we would have lost her either way."

"If your daughter is dead, you will do just fine." Mina walked toward the feeble woman and toward the path to the power she craved. With the neuromancer in her control, nothing would stop her meteoric rise.

"No, Mikyal, I think I'd rather be with my daughter than serve as your prisoner."

Mina hesitated as the woman drew forth a knife from her sleeve, the metal glinting in the light. Faster than Mina could react, Shamira drove it—

"NO!" Mina screamed as she ripped the memory away, tore it to pieces. She felt sobs echoing from her. She heard Gam Gam's voice behind her. In front of her, Mikyal's eyes rolled to the back of his head. She wanted to stop, but she couldn't. She wasn't done.

She returned to the pond and pulled at the memories. She saw reports drop on her desk. Someone had found Kelis, and he had a daughter. A daughter as old as the day of Shamira's death. She saw the plan form, saw the small retinue of soldiers leave against the commanding officer's wishes. When she returned with the girl, it would not matter that she betrayed an order. She found the village, set up in the inn. Told her soldiers it was a resting spot. Then came the fabrication of the lie. The thief who stole from her. She took four soldiers with her when she left for the house. Two came with bloodhounds in case anyone tried to run away. She learned from the first visit, the failure with Shamira.

Her men forced the door open, and they stormed the house. She swept through the sitting room and the kitchen. A man opened the back door and entered the house, head held high. He was older, but she recognized him.

"Kelis," Mina said. He would know why she was here.

"Mikyal." He rubbed dirt from his hands onto his pants. "I don't remember inviting you over for dinner."

"I have no intention of staying that long. No need to waste time on formality, old friend. Hand over the girl. I know she's Shamira's daughter. We will leave you in peace."

"I don't know what you're talking about. I have no daughter."

"Don't play the fool with me. We have watched the house for days now. I know you have a daughter, the correct age to be Shamira's own. If she's not what I think, you have nothing to fear. She will be returned without harm." The alternative was left unsaid. Her men were trusted, but it was better to stay vague for now. No need to make things more difficult by inviting competition.

Kelis's eyes darkened, and his jaw clenched. He glanced over one shoulder to the pumpkin patch in the back. A young girl of twelve stood there, eyes wide with fear. Had she always looked like a frightened animal? "Dear, you'll have to run!" he called over his shoulder.

"Move!" Mina, the one who was Mikyal, yelled. She pushed her way forward, but the scrawny man blocked her way. Her men rushed into the room with her yell.

"Run!" Kelis grunted as he pushed against his daughter's pursuer. "I know it'll be scary, but you have to run."

Mina drew her knife. Enough with distractions! She would have what she wanted. Mina plunged the blade into Kelis's torso as he looked over at his daughter. Through the ribs and into the heart. A quick death for an old friend.

The girl bolted, quick as a rabbit, into the woods beyond the pumpkins. Mina pushed at her friend, but his grip held firm. He clung to life even now that death was certain. She shook at him, and when he still failed to die, she turned back to her men.

"Chase her, you idiots. Into the woods! Get the hounds and chase her!" Her friend died in her arms, but not before two soldiers and the hounds set out into the woods on the girl's tail. The evening sun lowered itself over the treetops as Kelis's body collapsed to the ground.

Mina collapsed too as she pulled free from the last of the memories. Two arms caught her before she hit the ground. Papa looked down at her with fear, *real* fear, in his eyes. Gam Gam was there too, a hand to one cheek.

"She'll be fine," Gam Gam said, but her voice was so far away. "We must leave now though. I can't hold the spell much longer."

Papa lifted Mina into his arms, and Sloughy pulled Gam Gam to her feet. The necromancer walked arm in arm with the zombie. Gerald no longer put himself together. He had gone still, all animated life removed from him. The knitted hat still warmed his skull, and lifeless eye sockets stared up at the ceiling. The scarf was tangled among the pile of bones. They left him, the last of the dead carrying the living from the room.

Mina looked back and saw Mikyal on the ground, his body shaking with seizures, and more tears ran from her eyes. She would have thought they'd run dry at some point, but she always found more. She sobbed into her father's shoulder as she bounced in his arms.

The pounding of fists on doors echoed through the hallways like thunder and beat in rhythm with Mina's head. Exhaustion dragged her closer to sleep, her vision fading in and out as tears dried on her cheeks. She rocked in her father's arms and clung to consciousness as if dangling at the edge of a cliff. If she gave in, she knew she would regret it.

Gam Gam weaved around cluttered furniture jammed against the shuddering doors and decrepit bodies of the once unliving, and Papa followed. She walked steadier, but Sloughy still supported much of her weight. Mina wondered why the undead had become inactive since they had not encountered any additional soldiers.

Mina's focus faltered as her mind wandered, and she slipped into a dream, finding herself trapped within a locked room. Faceless undead piled furniture against the door as she pounded and yelled. The room shrank as she scrambled to escape, but the door wouldn't budge.

Fear jolted Mina awake, and she gasped at the sudden shock of consciousness that flooded back into her. As the haze cleared, Mina noticed they had started descending the final flight of stairs. Sloughy no longer supported Gam Gam, instead the necromancer walked on her own with head held high. They entered the common room where a few soldiers rose from the crumbled remains of their captors. Though the staff had also been released, they stayed where they were.

How had they escaped the undead?

"Stop them!" a soldier shouted, and those that could move grabbed at their weapons where possible and at random furniture or sturdy bones otherwise.

"That would not be wise," Gam Gam said, her voice strong and steady once more. A hint of the scolding, grandmotherly tone weaved into her words, stopping the soldiers in their tracks. She pulled out her mage's medallion. "I am a mage, sanctioned by the Eternal Empire. In discussions with your sergeant, it has become clear that Mina was unfairly suspected of thievery, and the charges have been dropped. Unfortunately, Sergeant Mikyal was also struck with a seizure and requires medical assistance I cannot provide. I've freed you to help him as a form of trust. I do not wish your sergeant dead, and I think neither do you."

The freed soldiers, five in total, including Bicep Woman, stared, makeshift weapons at the ready. Two made to advance, but then Bicep Woman raised a hand, halting them.

"The sergeant comes first. But if we find treachery has been done to him by your hand, we will not rest until justice is served."

"We will be in the wagon next to the cemetery," Gam Gam said, her tone pleasant, but the soldiers shivered as they looked at the undead around them, no doubt made uneasy by the power displayed.

Bicep Woman nodded and then led the others up the stairs past Mina and her father. Gam Gam took the opportunity to lead Sloughy and Papa out of the inn. The burning of Mina's head dulled as the cool breeze flowed between her hair and across her face.

Mina expected a horse ride next, a quick escape with Sebastian and Nora before the soldiers learned the agreement with Mikyal was no more than a mind wipe and dash. But two large piles of bones greeted them at the inn's broken-down door. Mina recognized the skulls and knew they belonged to the horses, inanimate once more. Just like the undead in the hallway and Gerald. And those in the common room.

"Gam Gam..." Mina asked in a hoarse whisper. "What's happening?"

"It's nothing, dear. We should keep moving." Gam Gam's labored breathing returned, and her shoulders slumped. Sloughy placed an arm around her for support once more.

For the second time, Mina unintentionally dozed, and this time it was longer before she could pull herself free from the dreams. When she woke again, they had arrived at the wagon. Gam Gam directed Papa to place her within. The commands were urgent, which caused Mina to worry. Was she hurt? Did using her power so much cause something to happen to her mind?

Gam Gam and Sloughy opened the doors, and the necromancer climbed in. "It should be around here," she mumbled as she pulled open drawers, kicking junk out of the way.

Papa set her against the wall beside the doorway. Mina was grateful since sitting made it easier to stay awake. Maybe that was why he had done so.

"Gam Gam..."

"Rest for now, Mina. Save your energy."

"What's happening?"

"I'm looking for something to help with your drowsiness is all, dear."

"Why..." Mina had to gather her breath to continue. "Why are you in a hurry?"

Gam Gam glanced at her, a dark gloom crossing her face, and her eyes shied away from Mina. Then she turned back to the drawers. Mina thought she saw tears on Gam Gam's cheeks. "I'm so sorry, Mina," she whispered. "I was supposed to be the one to protect you. That's what being an adult is supposed to mean. But you ended up saving me.

I'm sorry I put so much burden on your shoulders." She pulled a vial of green liquid from a drawer and brought it to Mina. It had an illegible label, the ink long ago worn off. "Take this dear, and we'll talk more."

Gam Gam sat on the edge of the wagon with a grunt. She closed her eyes, and her face sagged with exhaustion. The necromancer seemed as tired as Mina. She tipped the contents of the vial into her mouth and swallowed.

Its effects were instantaneous. A vibration of energy pulsed through her body, and a faint taste of dirt hung in her mouth. A flash of memory returned at the sensation, though it was not her own. It was of Mikyal and his use of vitamancy. The potion was a product of his kind of magic, which soured her taste of it. Regardless, strength returned to her limbs and wakefulness to her eyes and mind. She was no longer hampered as if her thoughts were pushed through syrup, no longer cold as if in a snowstorm. She knew she was still tired, but she was more awake than she had been in what seemed like ages.

"Mina," Gam Gam spoke, but her eyes were closed. Her focus held elsewhere. "I'm sorry for this, dear, I had hoped for more time, but this is the extent of my powers. Perhaps I am not very good, as you said. Inexperienced can also mean overconfident."

"What's wrong, Gam Gam?" Panic pushed Mina's heart faster and faster. Her chest clenched against her breath.

"The spell will not hold much longer. The vial I gave you should keep you awake to say your goodbyes." Tears flowed from Gam Gam's closed eyes, and Mina felt her own following suit.

"Goodbyes?"

"To your father. I'm sorry, my power is demanding my attention, and the right words are taking too long to come to me. I'll hold for a few more minutes at least, but then your father will have to return beyond the Veil." As if on cue, a soft thud emitted from beside the wagon as Sloughy collapsed into nothing but rotten flesh. "No arguments, dear, I can only do so much. You have your chance to say goodbye, you should take it."

Mina looked to her father, who watched her closely from nearby. "Why?" Mina's words turned to sobs, and through her sobs she blurted, "Why? Why didn't you take the vial so you could have the energy?"

"It wouldn't have worked. The vial doesn't heal, just helps with attentiveness. The spell would still have failed, and *you* would have been asleep for it."

Papa stepped forward and placed a hand on Mina's arm. She fell into his chest, the pain tearing open her heart once again. She screamed out, and Papa ran a hand through her hair. She held her father's corpse close while it still remembered her. "Tomorrow? Can you bring him back tomorrow? Just like today?"

"It is a powerful spell that creates a tether between the soul and the body for a short time. It cannot be performed more than once for each soul without risking irreversible damage. I—" Gam Gam's voice cut out with her own stifled sob. "I can't bring him back again."

Mina clung harder to her father than ever before, as if to hold his soul by her own strength. His arms were gentle around her in return. "Papa," Mina said. Her words choked her as they all tried to race out at once. She had to choose one thing at a time, the most important first. It was a struggle to push them out. "I don't want you to go, Papa. I want you to stay with me. I want to see the sea with you. I want you to see me grow up. I don't want you to go!"

Papa pulled Mina from the hug, and she looked into his eyes. A tear rolled from one, something that should have been impossible. He raised a finger to his eye and then pointed at Mina as if to say, *I'll be watching you, always.*

"I don't know how to do anything without you, Papa!" Mina wiped at her eyes, and new tears quickly replaced those wiped away. "I don't know what to do. I can't go on without you. It hurts too much. Please don't leave again!"

Papa's own hand brushed against Mina's cheek, then he nodded toward Gam Gam. *She will help you.* He smiled to assure her, but Mina felt only panic and fear.

"Papa." She sniffed her insufferable runny nose. "Papa, I love you. I love you so much!"

Papa opened his mouth, and a single word rumbled from within him. Another impossibility. The greatest communication from the undead had always been grunts and groans. The precision for words was beyond their capabilities. Gam Gam's eyes opened wide in surprise. She would come to tell Mina that there has never been a recorded instance of an undead speaking any intelligible word.

But Mina's father did so to pass one last message to his daughter.

"Love."

Then he grew heavy in Mina's arms. "Papa? Papa!" The body slid from her grasp to the ground below. "Papa!" But her father grew still on the cold dirt just outside the village's cemetery.

"I'm sorry," Gam Gam said, her own tears running fast down her cheeks. "I'm so sorry." Gam Gam pulled Mina into an embrace as they both cried. "I'm sorry, Mina," she said again, then both were silent besides their soft sobs and sniffles. Exhaustion overtook their grief, and sleep soon came for Mina and Gam Gam.

Mina woke once in the night when Nugget returned. His bare bones made soft clacks against the wood floor as he curled up next to Mina and nuzzled against her. Mina cuddled the skeletal cat and fell asleep once more.

9

They buried Mina's father the next morning. Gam Gam had risen Sloughy with a simple animation spell to restore him as he was. The zombie found a shovel and began work on clearing out the grave. Mina and Gam Gam were still far too exhausted to do much, and since Sloughy did not tire, he was more than happy to do the bulk of the work. Mina sat on the ground and watched the methodical process, her father's hand held tight in her own.

The question she wanted to ask sat in her throat, but fear choked it back down even as she tried to force it out. Soul tethering wouldn't be an option, but was there another way?

Sloughy cleared the last of the dirt, and time ran out. She pushed the words out, her voice quaking. "What about resurrection?"

"What?" Gam Gam looked surprised, her attention pulled from wherever it had lingered. "Resurrection?"

"Like with your grandkids. Why can't we resurrect Papa?"

She knew what the answer would be, if not why it had to be. Because if it was an option, Gam Gam would have said something. The necromancer's face answered better than any words. Her eyes shifted away to look at the ground near Papa's feet.

"It wouldn't work," she said. Her voice started low and quiet but gained strength and volume as she continued. "Not how you would want it to. The afterlife affects the soul, which makes it a challenge to return to this world. Even a tether puts a strain on it, and that's more like creating a bridge to reach across the Veil. The soul doesn't fully return here. To bring one back completely, it would need to be reactive and malleable. Able to adjust to the shock of living once more.

"This is easier with kids than adults." Her words ran together with practiced ease. "Adult minds are set in their ways, whereas kids can adjust to trauma; they can change as they age. It might be difficult to start, but in a year, maybe two, it will be like the death never happened."

"It's not fair!"

Mina screamed the words, and Gam Gam jumped, her eyes wide. Morning birds screeched into the cool air and took flight. Mina was surprised at her own voice, like pressure had built within her until it popped. Popped like... like Sir Gibblet. She forced her voice down even as she wanted to scream more. Wanted to shake the necromancer, to break crates and bottles and whatever she could get her hands on.

"It's not fair. Why should you get your grandkids and I get nothing?"

"I'm so sorry, dear. I—"

"I don't want you to be sorry! I want my papa!"

Gam Gam's gaze shifted away from her again, looking elsewhere, or perhaps nowhere. But Mina saw the pain as the woman's eyes shifted, and a flurry of guilt sank into her, even as her grief and anger overwhelmed it.

"I can't work miracles, Mina. If I could, I would. I would do anything to save you from this pain. You just have to trust that I know my magic, and I am doing the very best that I can."

Mina cradled her father's arm, then buried her face into his chest. Tears ran hot down her cheeks and onto the sweater. Gam Gam tried to say more, but Mina didn't listen. She held her father and let her emotions out. When she pulled away, Sloughy was ready to take her father from her forever.

The funeral was simple. Sloughy lowered Papa into the grave, and Mina watched because it would be her last opportunity to see him. She was given the chance to throw the first dirt on, then Sloughy filled in the grave. Mina watched through blurry vision, her eyes never wavering from the spot where her father would lie forever.

When the zombie finished, Gam Gam presented Mina with a stake torn from the cemetary's fence—and a knife. Mina took to the task with singular focus, pouring everything she had into it. Though it didn't look as professional as the headstones, it was made by her hand and by her love. She wrote, "Kelis, husband of Shamira and father of Mina. The greatest to live twice." Sloughy helped her place the marker, and she spent a moment more standing at the grave, unsure of what else to do.

Gam Gam stepped beside her and placed a hand on her shoulder. "I must go collect the horses, but if you—"

Mina didn't wait to hear more. She stormed off to the wagon and slammed the door shut behind her. She curled up by the stove, huddled into a blanket, and cried. When she wasn't crying, she stared at the wall, her mind numb to the world around her. Nugget coiled in her lap, and Mina absentmindedly stroked the undead cat.

There was a knock and a call of, "Mina dear, do you need anything before we head out?" But Mina ignored it, and soon enough the wagon moved on, leaving her father behind.

The soldiers never pursued. In the days to come, Gam Gam would explain that when she returned for the horses, Sergeant Mikyal had no recollection of Mina or her, and could find no evidence of thievery, and any suspicious gaps in his memory seemed to be attributed to the seizure. Thus, he called off the hunt. The soldiers, though still suspicious, were more than willing to let it go when it was revealed new orders had arrived which demanded their return. Beyond the one broken nose, no harm had been done, and so the matter was dropped.

Mina's mind wipe had worked and would protect them for now. This success didn't make her feel better.

For a week, they traveled west. Gam Gam had recovered the bones of Gerald in addition to Sebastian and Nora. The soldiers had decided not to leave the corpses around the inn, and instead stacked them in the alley for disposal. It had made Gam Gam's job easier with all the pieces in one place. She even took the time to animate the other corpses long enough to return them to the graveyard for the townsfolk.

On the road, the undead took over the typical tasks of setting up and tearing down camp while the living recovered. Although within a day Mina felt better physically, her mood made her sluggish and unresponsive. Gam Gam continued to use the branch as a cane, though she became more surefooted each passing day.

The illusory gems were returned, and the horses looked alive once more. It helped to avoid awkward questions as they passed through villages and towns. Sloughy and Gerald spent most of their time hidden within the wagon for the same reason, making the cramped area smell rancid and driving Mina to sulk on the driver's bench beside Gam Gam. Mina suspected that was the necromancer's intention.

Gam Gam was ceaseless in her attempts to distract and comfort. She would talk about her time at the academy.

About the other students, a fraction her age, and the odd and sometimes hilarious accidents she caused in her practice. She talked about meeting Nugget, and mentioned how those lacking natural magical gifts could still find their way to gaining magic themselves. It was a more difficult path, but it also allowed one to start wherever they wished.

She prodded Mina with questions and games. In one such attempt to distract, Gam Gam tried to teach Mina how to knit. The lessons ended when a pair of needles, and the yarn they were attached to, were tossed into a tree as Mina yelled in frustration at a dropped stitch and a tangled mess.

During that week, Mina had her good days and her bad. Now safe from danger, her grief boiled within her, a monster clawing to escape and aggravated all the more by the second loss of her father. She felt like a raw wound picked back open. But that was better than when she felt like a black abyss of nothing, leaching all the happiness and color from around her. When she was like that, none of Gam Gam's words could reach her. The necromancer stayed by her side through it all. She baked cookies and knitted Mina mittens to warm her against the dropping temperatures. What clothes they had not salvaged from Mina's home before their exodus were purchased in the next town over. She was grateful for the warm clothing and felt guilty for not knowing how to express it.

Each night, Mina lay awake well past dark, staring at the roof. She listened for the sounds of Gam Gam's soft breathing to know the old woman had fallen asleep. Then, from around her neck, she pulled out her parents' rings and held them in her hands. She whispered to them, careful not to wake Gam Gam, and told them about her day. She pretended they were messengers straight to her parents. She asked them for help each day. The pain was too much, and she wanted nothing more than to see them both one more time. One more day. She asked if they were proud of her. Proud that she was able to help with baking. She wasn't very good and burned the entire first batch, but Gam Gam told her it was trickier than it looked, and it would take practice. The second batch was even edible.

She hoped wherever her parents were, they could hear her stories. They could know that someone was caring for their daughter. She missed them, but she was never alone.

Several days passed before Mina had the courage to ask about Sir Gibblet. Gam Gam smiled this time and told Mina not to worry about him. He would be at peace for the first time in over a century. Gam Gam had saved him from his afterdeath as a revenant, and he had chosen to ignore his Call to cross the Veil. His soul had been tortured and twisted by his tenure as a vengeful spirit, and he would not have been able to rest until he left their world. He would be enjoying the comforts of the afterlife and healing and reuniting with family. Gam Gam was sure of Sir Gibblet's happiness and hoped there were many scarves for him to wear. Sir Gibblet had been especially fond of her scarves.

Mina accepted that as a small comfort for the loss of a friend. She wouldn't want him to be in pain, and he deserved peace after so long fighting. So it was just the two of them. Well, there was Nugget, and Sloughy and Gerald of course. Though the undead were never much for conversation. Not that Mina minded. At the moment, she was not much for conversation either.

Just when Mina thought she was getting better, she would be catatonic the next day, all thought of food making her nauseous. She was tempted with her favorites: cinnamon cookies for treats, cheddar biscuits and potatoes for a meal. Guilt continued to dig into her stomach, telling her she was useless, and Gam Gam would give up on her soon. Mina knew she would never be abandoned, but on her worst days the fear would fester in her head. It would tell her she wasn't enough. Just a replacement until Gam Gam's grandkids returned. Then she would be too much work. It would be easier to leave her behind.

She hated these thoughts. She wanted to be better and told herself company her age would help. She tried to think positively about the new kids, but some irrationality still dug at her, still unnerved her. Even on her good days.

It was a good day when they arrived at the seaside cliff. The sun dripped from its peak, and Mina's mood was better than it had been since her father's deaths. Excitement bloomed within her like a single flower on a rocky out-cropping. The feeling was strange after so long battling her black grief, but thoughts of beautiful sunsets and blue water returned some cheer to her.

Gam Gam had parked the wagon at the edge of a thinly wooded area, which butted up against a hill. A pathway snaked up the incline, and Mina could hear the crashing of the sea beyond. The air tasted of salt and smelled of brine. Mina helped pack a pair of meals, and together they set off on the path by foot. The undead were left with the wagon. Nugget curled up on a bundle of blankets in Gerald's lap, and the skeletal human set about scratching at a spot behind the skeletal cat's nonexistent ear.

The sea would be blocked from view until they reached the edge of the cliff, and Mina vibrated with the excitement of something new. Gam Gam, still exhausted from the overexertion of her powers and from general old age, struggled up the path. Their progress was slow, and Mina forced herself to calm down and keep pace with the necromancer. At least until the necromancer shooed her off with a smile, and Mina sprinted the rest of the way.

Mina's eyes burst wide when more and more of the sea appeared. She stood at the edge of the cliff and stared out at the endless blue stretching out before her. She could do nothing but gawk, a wide smile on her face. She squinted in search of land on the other side but couldn't find any.

"It must go on forever!" she shouted to Gam Gam as the old woman crested the hill.

Gam Gam chuckled as she joined Mina. "It's not forever, but it's certainly a long way."

Mina looked around at the flat clearing atop the cliff and spotted the gravestones to their left. They were the only obstructions to an otherwise empty area. Three in a row, one for the parents and one for each child. Gam Gam grew quiet as they approached, her grin replaced with a solemn look, the lines of her face pulling her mouth into a frown. The sun dipped toward the horizon and morphed the headstones' shadows into one long streak.

"Are you ready?" Mina asked.

Gam Gam laughed, but the sound was devoid of her usual cheer. "I'm supposed to be the one to ask you that."

"But I have nothing to be ready for."

"I know." She looked at the graves for a long moment and took a deep breath. "I thought I'd be more ready after waiting so long, but it is harder than I thought."

Mina nodded and stepped back, giving Gam Gam the time she needed to work out the spell. She clutched the basket of sandwiches tight to her chest, and it creaked in distress from Mina's anxious grip.

Gam Gam breathed in and raised her hands as she had for the soul tethering spell. Mina frowned a little, wondering how this spell would be different. It had to be different.

The nagging feeling returned, and Mina tried to push it away. But Mikyal's words still bounced around her skull. Would Gam Gam's necromancy be enough to bring them back? She shook her head free of the negativity. Gam Gam knew what she was doing. There was nothing wrong. It was just the prospect of getting along with her grandkids that made Mina nervous. That was all.

The necromancer's head rose to the sky, and Mina prepared for the winds to pick up. Gam Gam remained that way for a long moment, tension rising with each passing second. Then she dropped to the ground. Not in a heap, but on her rump in an awkward seated position. Her hands came up to her face, and Mina heard a faint whimper.

Mina bolted to the woman, throwing the basket to one side, fear clenching her heart in its unrelenting grip. "Gam Gam!" She knelt beside the necromancer and looked at her face. Tears streamed down her cheeks as her hands fell away. "Did something go wrong?" Mina looked around for signs of the spell's failure but didn't know what to look for. It seemed as though the spell hadn't even begun.

Gam Gam sniffed, and then she sighed. "No, dear." She paused for a moment as she brushed her tears away. She took in another deep breath and continued. "I just wanted to see their faces one more time, you know? It's been so long."

Mina understood, more than she wished, and it had only been a week since her father. For Gam Gam it had been so much longer. But she didn't understand what Gam Gam meant or why that would stop the spell, so she stayed silent. Anxiety crawled up from her stomach to her chest, burning the entire way.

Gam Gam stared at the two graves for several breaths before speaking again. "But, I can't do it. They left this world too soon, and that is a great tragedy. But it would be far worse to put them through the pain of returning. The pain of existing in that state. It wouldn't be true life; they wouldn't grow, or need to eat, or live at all, really. That is not my gift to give. It's no easier for kids. I just blinded myself from that for my own selfish desire. I cannot force that on anyone. Especially not my little babies."

Mina remained frozen, unsure of what to do. She had never faced anyone else's grief. But Gam Gam *had* helped her, and so Mina tried to remember what Gam Gam did. Cautiously, Mina placed a hand on Gam Gam's back. "I understand."

Gam Gam let out a laugh, which turned into a sob. "Of course you do, dear. I'm telling you everything you just went through." Her eyes remained glued to those two tiny graves. "I'm sorry. I shouldn't have returned. I just wanted to see them one more time. But not like this."

Mina couldn't stop the pain, no one could. But she could do one thing for Gam Gam. She knew how now. She understood enough, she was sure of it. Even so, her breathing came fast, and panic beat her heart like a drum. Again, she fell back to her breathing exercises, a gift from her father. Long deep breaths, in, then out. She closed her eyes to focus, cutting away the sensory input around her as much as possible. The salt from the sea blew onto her lips, and she tasted it. The wind blew her hair around, tickling against her cheek and brow. She smelled the earth and the grass. Her heart slowed, and her panic withdrew. She *could* do it.

Mina reached out with her power. Gam Gam's mind appeared clear to her, filled with the roiling dark blue of grief. Like the gentle currents of a stream, her magic reached out for Gam Gam's mind. Not like the crushing power she had wielded twice before. Not with the intent of destruction, but instead creation. She understood what she did to destroy the memory, and so she understood how to avoid that.

Gam Gam looked at her with curiosity, surely feeling the touch of Mina's power at this distance. Mina met her gaze and saw no fear in the woman's eyes. She would never be afraid of Mina, she had promised so. Mina's eyes watered, but she smiled. She reached out and took hold of one hand, gripping it tight between both of hers. Gam Gam squeezed back.

"Think of your grandchildren, Gam Gam," Mina said as she channeled the confidence the old woman placed in her. "Your favorite moments."

Gam Gam nodded and turned her attention to the gravestones as she took a deep breath. Mina delved into the necromancer's mind with a soft touch.

Grandchildren.

Gam Gam's mind filled with memories. Hundreds, if not thousands, of the petals drifted to the surface. Mina's reach was cautious and gentle. Not an iron grip, but rather a brush of a finger through hair. She focused on them one at a time, avoiding the pull, like a flame, to consume and overwhelm. She watched the memories as if they were moving paintings rather than experiencing them as her own. She could see them and remember them, and so she projected from her own mind without pulling from Gam Gam's. The memories remained intact. A careful balance that now felt intuitive after Mina's previous disasters.

The images blossomed above the gravestones. Babes no older than a week held in arms. Birthdays and holidays, picnics beneath beautiful sunsets coloring the sky in different shades of pink, purple, and orange.

Gam Gam watched the memories play out in silence, new tears following the tracks of the old, one hand covering her mouth as the other tightened in Mina's grip. Young Asher kicked a ball that little Evelyn chased, both giggling the entire time. Smiling without a worry in the world. Pure happiness manifested into two little children.

Mina continued through the memories, each playing out for their few moments before moving to the next. She searched for the right memory. Something recent. Something still. She found it in a memory of the very same cliff where they sat now. Gam Gam asked the kids to stand still to let her get a look at them. Asher, with an arm wrapped around his little sister's shoulders, smiled up at his grandmother while Evelyn hooked two fingers in her mouth and pulled her lips apart, showing off a gap in her teeth. The silly look sent all three giggling.

The images faded from above the graves, and disappointment crossed Gam Gam's face though she tried to hide it. Mina closed her eyes against that disappointment, and she smiled as she took in one more deep breath.

It was said that the greatest neuromancers could not only create illusions but could also reach into another's mind and pull objects of great desire from within them. This was the ability that gave them the moniker of djinn and made them wealthy once upon a time. Before they were hunted for what else their powers could accomplish. Mina understood this process now. It came to her as intuitively as her projections. It was not unlike creating an illusion, just more substantial. She couldn't make it live, not like a vitamancer's abilities, but she could still *create*.

She concentrated her energy on the manifestation. Not just an image projected into the air, but something solid. A small, square plate of ethereal stone formed in front of Gam Gam. It was nothing special in structure, which made it easy for Mina to craft, but the one face would hold the exact likeness of two small children staring out. One with a big smile, the other with a goofy grin and a missing tooth. It would never fade and never crack.

The power strained within Mina, stretching her further than ever before. Her breath became ragged, and sweat bathed her temples. But she remembered Gam Gam in that moment before her father died the second time. She remembered how hard the necromancer pushed herself to allow Mina the goodbye she needed. Mina pushed harder. She focused on that image and manifested it. She would not give up after everything Gam Gam had done for her.

When it was complete, Mina slumped forward and caught herself with weak arms, gasping for breath. She looked over to Gam Gam, watching as trembling hands picked up the memory made solid. A sob wracked the grandmother's body, and then another. Gam Gam wept into one hand as the memory trembled in her other.

Worry snaked its way back within Mina. She thought she had done it perfectly. Did she mess up? Did she ruin the memory? Her own hands shook at the fear of causing irreparable damage. "Did I do something wrong?" she cried. "I—I can fix it if it's wrong. I think I can. I just—I need a little rest, and I can try again. Please, I didn't ruin anything, did I?" Mina couldn't stop her own tears now. She had never seen Gam Gam so upset before. Never seen *anyone* so sad.

But Gam Gam shook her head so hard a few tears fell to Mina's trousers. Then she smiled the biggest smile Mina had seen yet. "No, Mina. It's perfect."

Gam Gam pulled her into a hug with all her strength. A thousand thank yous rang from her mouth as she squeezed Mina hard. A flood of joy and warmth ran through Mina and washed away her anxiety. She had done it right, and for the first time in days, she felt the cold chill of dread and depression leave her as she returned the hug. She wept with Gam Gam, but this was different somehow. Not the screaming pain she had felt, but something warmer. Tears she didn't mind shedding.

The two held each other and shared their mourning and their stories. For hours they told tales, Mina of her father and Gam Gam of her family. They laughed, and they cried. No longer alone in the world, their grief had found comfort in one another, and the darkness brightened if only a little.

They ate their dinner with the setting sun and dried their tears with the laughter of remembrance. When they rose to leave, Gam Gam spent a few moments with the graves in silent farewell. Mina watched the sea, the white foam rolling in on waves. When she was ready, Gam Gam joined Mina, and they watched the stars and the moon reflected in those dark waters.

"Do you want to see the town where they lived?" Gam Gam asked. "It's just off the beach and has wonderful swimming."

"I've never been swimming. Is it scary?"

"For a girl as brave as you? Not at all." Gam Gam stared at her for another long moment. "You're just like my grand-kids, you know. With that brave, kind heart and big brain of yours."

Mina blushed at the compliment and shrugged. "Well, you're a lot like my parents. Strong, protective, and one of the most selfless people in the world. I wouldn't be here without you."

Gam Gam laughed and said, "And I don't think I'd be here without you."

Mina knew the grief would always be there, the pain would never leave forever, and knew Gam Gam felt the same. But she thought maybe, with time, and with some-one else there to share the hard moments, there would come a day when they both would be all right again.

The Knight Revenant

Adam Holcombe

bountyink.com

The Knight Revenant

In the desolate lands between two cities, an elderly woman sat knitting on a stool. A blight haunted the realm—a revenant left over from a war a century ago—laying waste and leaving death wherever it went. It was said that none had crossed its domain and survived. It was said that to travel into the wastes meant certain death. All this and more was told to the elderly woman. All this and more was ignored.

Gam Gam camped in the wastelands near her horse-drawn wagon, the bones of a cat curled up at her feet. Death did not stop the cat from being annoyed when the old woman tugged a small hat onto his head. He hissed at her, though without the required flesh, the hiss was silent. He clacked his teeth instead.

"Aw, Nugget, you're so adorable in your hat," Gam Gam said as she pulled the cap more snuggly onto Nugget. Noting the fit, she removed it and began the cast off. Her eyes glanced up only once at the encroaching mist that defied the hot afternoon sun. In a louder voice, Gam Gam said, "If you attack me, you won't like the results much."

Nugget looked up at the old woman, a look of surprise not quite showing on his face (given the absence of a face), though, the added way he crooked his head did wonders to portray his confusion. Then Nugget turned to stare at the gray mist of spectral energy that rolled up to their camp. Strands of mist suddenly formed into tendrils, stabbing at the woman with blinding speed.

They slammed against an invisible barrier—unable to reach Gam Gam or anything else within the camp—and startled Nugget. A terrible sparking and a scream of agony filled the empty space. Nugget watched with curiosity as the tendrils withdrew.

Gam Gam was a necromancer—a terribly talented one, at that—and after tales of an ancient horror surfaced during a visit to a nearby city, she set out to investigate. She was not the kind of person who could sit around idly while others could be endangered, not when she had the power to change it.

"Told you." She finished the cast off, set the completed hat aside, and looked the new arrival straight on. Or as straight on as one could when it comes to a phantasmal cloud. Its misty form spread out and encircled the campsite entirely, two glowing eyes lit with rage floated within the densest fog. Gam Gam's soul barrier crackled whenever it drifted too close. "Calm down, I've dealt with toddlers before. A temper tantrum will not bother me."

The revenant answered with a deafening roar, and the tendrils of mist speared toward her once again. When the barrier refused to budge against the assault, it growled until the very land rumbled.

"Did you want to talk about it?"

Apparently, it did not. The revenant receded into the distance instead, hiding among the dead trees and deep ravines. Its stare prickled at her neck, and the waves of malice and hatred that wafted from it curdled her stomach. A foreboding sense of duty invaded her thoughts, a duty to stop anyone from crossing.

"I'll be here when you want to talk!"

As night fell, Gam Gam packed away her stool and her new project, this one a pair of socks—well, just the one sock to start anyway. She made great progress with the absence of the revenant, already she was finished with the heel turn and working her way down the foot. She threw dirt on the fire, climbed into the wagon, set out her bedroll, and slipped within.

It was not long before the crackling of the barriers woke her. Gam Gam rose with a yawn, put on a pair of slippers, and stepped back out into the cool night. Nugget raised his head for only a moment before returning to his nap atop the small stove built into the wagon.

The revenant surrounded the camp in a semisphere, maybe even a full sphere if it had found a way underground. That didn't matter, however, since the soul barrier encompassed the camp in that direction as well. The moon was a shaded glow through the shroud of mist.

For a long moment the revenant pushed inward from every direction at once, and wild energy exploded around her. Then the mist jerked back as if shocked, which Gam Gam supposed it was—though she couldn't say quite what reaction the barrier produced since it only affected the undead.

"I'm afraid you won't find much use in brute force. I haven't been at this long," —In fact, Gam Gam had been at this (this being necromancy in an official capacity) for twenty-two days, four hours, and thirty-four minutes, after having graduated top of her class from the mage's academy in Capital City— "but I know what I'm doing. That barrier will hold just fine. I am happy to talk if you'd like to, however."

It screeched at her, a high-pitched whine that tore at Gam Gam's ears and drove into her head like a knitting needle into the thumb. Her hands clapped to her ears, though proved useless to stop the scream's assault. Eventually it died down, and able to hear her own thoughts again, Gam Gam cocked an eyebrow at the mist.

"Was that really necessary?"

The revenant sulked away back into the darkness, and Gam Gam returned to her wagon and slept through the rest of the night without issue.

The revenant was waiting across the barrier the next morning. The two burning eyes watched as Gam Gam ran through her routine. After breakfast, she pulled out her knitting and started again. Still, the revenant did nothing but watch and radiate rage. Gam Gam ignored it.

A wave of satisfaction washed over the necromancer, not her own, and she glanced up at the revenant. For a moment, wisps of mist curled upward, almost as if to smile, then the fog shifted to surround the barrier. Gam Gam returned to knitting with a sigh—it would learn soon enough it couldn't get through.

The light dulled as the revenant rose over the top, and then faded further as energy pulsed through its misty form. The fog thickened as it summoned more strength. A century of hatred fueled the revenant, and Gam Gam felt it pour every little bit it could into its nebulous body, solidifying until—

"Really?" Gam Gam sighed in the newly formed darkness. "Was that necessary? Now I lost count of my stitches."

She rose and carefully made her way to the wagon, arms held in front of her. She grumbled as she kicked something, and grumbled more as the something clawed her back. "Knock it off, Nugget, I can't see." She returned with a lit lantern in one hand and an angry cat skeleton stalking behind her.

"And how long can you keep up this new trick?" Gam Gam asked as she settled back into her chair, picking the unfinished sock up once more. The revenant did not respond. An hour later (still in darkness) Gam Gam added, "That's actually quite impressive. Must have saved up a lot of negativity for a moment like this."

The revenant growled.

"Be careful, I think that was almost a word! You *can* tell me what has upset you whenever you wish, you know."

"Kill you." The words rolled through the camp with their own force, the lantern's flame flickering in the aftermath.

"Well, for one, I'd rather you didn't," Gam Gam said. Her eyes strained against the lantern light to continue her knitting. She wasn't ready to confront the spirit yet, she needed it to be ready to listen, and to talk. She had time, though. The barrier would hold for many more days. "For two, I highly doubt your desire to kill me started this. I'm old, but not that old. I wasn't even alive when you died."

It roared, then light filled the camp again and Gam Gam shielded her eyes against the sudden brightness. When she could see again, the revenant was gone. But it had spoken, and soon, she would be able to connect with it. That was progress. For now, she had her knitting.

"Not a very civilized spirit, is it?" Gam Gam asked Nugget. The skeletal cat responded only with a glare.

Gam Gam knitted in peace for many hours, approaching the toe of her first sock: a bright orange and purple garment with cabling at its cuff to give it a pleasant texture. Nugget eventually stopped sulking and returned to his spot atop the stove. Lunch was made and eaten in quiet, as was dinner. Even the prickling sensation on her neck had disappeared. Had the revenant given up? Or did it just want her to think so?

She placed the partial sock within a small cloth bag, then returned it to the wagon. "Nugget, I'm going out for a bit to see if I can find that ghost, you stay here." Then she chuckled. "Well, it's not like you have a choice while the barrier is up."

Nugget raised his head indignantly, then returned to sleep.

Gam Gam walked to the edge of the barrier and, not feeling the sensation of being watched, stepped across. She waited several moments for the ambush, but it never came.

She circled the campsite, and checked beneath a bush that was only mostly dead. She looked down into a crag and saw only empty darkness, no foreboding sense of anguish or burning red eyes. She walked by the horses, and stepped within the barrier to give them a pat, then looked out at the barren wastes. She sighed.

With the lack of foliage, she could see far in all directions; only the few remaining trees, absent all leaves, still interrupted her sight. The land was dry and cracked, allowing for the gray dust to fly in the air with ease, which made spotting the other wagon effortless.

"Oh no." Gam Gam hiked up her skirts and ran toward the newcomer as fast as she could. Which wasn't very fast.

Kraya was one of two cities to flank the revenant's haunt. A hundred years prior, it had launched a war against the opposing city of Shelen, and though the war ravaged them both, Kraya was the one that suffered the most when it lost. Built at the top of a rocky cliff, it had little to no access to the waters which were filled with a magnitude of dangers for the inexperienced—and, often enough, experienced—sailor. The main road led through the wastes, and so traffic to and from the city disappeared in the revenant's wake.

With trade routes eviscerated, the city crumbled. Its farmlands were poor, its wellsprings nearly tapped out, its supplies nonexistent. The governor of Kraya had petitioned the Eternal Empire, its liege, for assistance for decades. But Kraya was destitute, and necromancers were rare and expensive. The longer a necromancer failed to take the job, the less Kraya had in its coffers to pay.

The city's death spiral was near its end when Gam Gam heard of the troubles in Shelen—the other flanking city, and the far more prosperous one. She talked to the governor, a short fellow from whom the scent of cheese wafted, and he agreed to provide assistance to the opposing city in the event the revenant was removed. But none in Kraya knew of her goals, and there were times where life grew desperate enough to take a risk.

And whoever was in the cart was desperate.

Gam Gam ran until her knees ached and her left hip forced her into a speedy waddle. She had a few choice words for whoever decided to cross the wastes. Mostly along the lines of "nincompoop" and "woolheaded fool." The nagging aches made it hard for her to remember that the citizens of Kraya did not know what she was doing. There was no way to send them word without crossing the wastes first. They could not be blamed for taking a risk deemed worthy when they were without information.

But then her back started aching, and the rude words returned to the forefront of her mind. She paused and leaned against a rock, gasping as if freshly pulled from the river. Like one of those...slimy animals? Those with the fins and the scales... Oh dear, her overtaxed body leached the energy from her mind, leaving her head empty except for the many complaints that bounced around within. Thinking was too difficult. The good news was the revenant had not shown itself yet, she had—

As if summoned by the very thought, the revenant rose from a ravine like smoke from a burnt cookie. The mist rolled across the lands in a billowing wave, crashing over and around the rocks and desiccated trees. Those in the wagon, several individuals from what she could see, panicked at the supernatural motion and tried to make the frightened donkey pull the cart harder. Instead, it kicked free, breaking the wagon in the process, and bolted away.

Their shouts glided across the land like stitches down a needle. Four distinct voices, two children. A boy and a girl. A father and a mother. Gam Gam's heart froze. Despite the heat, a chill ran through her that rooted her to the ground. For an instant, she heard her family's shouts of terror. Saw her family assaulted by the mists of a revenant.

Her sweet, little girl, all grown and married to a lovely, kind gentleman who was ready to help at a moment's notice. Two rambunctious children who captured her heart with tiny hands and soft giggles. They grew so big, she could hardly remember a time in which she had been able to hold them anymore.

For an instant, she almost broke. But her pains were driven from her mind by purpose. What of those kids' grandmother? What of their other family? She wouldn't let someone else suffer that loss.

Aches be damned, Gam Gam pulled at her sweater's collar—allowing the air to cool her down—she hiked up her skirts, and she ran on. Her knees hurt, a piercing pain that shot up and down her legs. Her hip didn't want to roll forward, creating a hitch in her step. She didn't care, as long as it got her to the revenant faster.

Any hopes that the revenant would give chase to the fleeing donkey were quashed immediately. Apparently animals did not fall under its obsession. The mother herded the kids under the cart, while the father swung a piece of wood at the encroaching clouds.

She couldn't see their faces, and so her mind interposed those of her own family's. She saw Wyatt through the fog, makeshift weapon raised against an incorporeal entity. No thoughts of fear for himself, only for his family. Kera huddled in front of the children, arms spread protectively against a force that could brush her aside with ease. Asher and Evelyn poked concerned heads out around their mother, tears falling from frightened eyes. She saw their deaths a hundred ways on her race to the cart.

Tendrils formed again, the same that battered against her soul barrier with such incredible force only the day before. Appendages that could tear a person in half. She heard the rumble of the revenant's growl, the land shaking with its words.

"None shall pass these lands!" The tendrils tore through the air and—

"Sir Gibblet!"

—they stopped short of the man, who fell to the ground quaking as his legs gave out. Gam Gam panted at the edge of the mist, her knees burned and her hip seized up. But she held herself straight and eyed the revenant.

The family's stares tracked to her and now that she was closer she couldn't imagine having mistaken them for her family. The differences were far greater than the similarities. Ages were wrong, skin tones were off, hair color was completely different. That didn't even take into account that it couldn't be her family out here. Not when... Gam Gam pushed the thought away. None of that mattered right now. She couldn't let anyone else lose their lives to the spirit of the wastes. To the phantom soldier consumed by anger. To the Knight Revenant.

The mist pulled away from the family and smothered her like a woolen blanket. The air around her blistered with heat, drenching her even further in sweat until she felt as though her clothing soaked through. The air thickened with rage and hatred. She wiped at her forehead, where her hair stuck down in a sodden mess.

"That is quite enough, don't you think?" she scolded the spirit as she reached into her pocket and picked out a small, circular medallion. Her secret weapon, as long as she could get the revenant to listen long enough. She had no choice but to make it listen now.

Beyond the mist, the father clawed his way to his family, where they huddled together, fear painting their eyes wide.

"How do you know who I am?" The revenant demanded. It spoke, that was good.

"Do you think I'm a fool who wanders into wastelands for fun? I know who you were, Knight Revenant. You were once a kindly man, and a gallant warrior. You have fallen far."

"Quiet, witch!" The revenant bellowed and the mist pressed in, suffocating her. "Do not speak to me of my life. I am the one who lived it. Then I was forced to live beyond it, endlessly tormented by my failures. You know *nothing*."

"I know that you kill innocents. Is that what you want to be remembered for? Sir Gibblet, the mighty knight who slaughtered children."

"Innocents? Never. There are only those who wish to cross the lands and continue the war—a war I have ended. To slaughter families like livestock. To kill children like bugs. My failure has been painted across the dirt with the blood of my family. Never shall I let these lands be crossed again."

Gam Gam gripped the medallion tighter. Not yet, he wouldn't believe her yet. "You seem to have some misconceptions about your failure."

"You will not deceive me with lies. You're here to banish me."

"If my goal was to banish you, I would have done that by now." The assaulting heat pricked her skin like a thousand needles. Her sweater hung heavy, and her lungs worked harder with each breath of oppressive fog. "But then your torment would never end. Your spirit would remain broken forever. You died in the war, in a last stand with your men. It takes a year for a revenant to form. What do you know of what followed your death?"

"We were overwhelmed. I was the last to die, you cannot trick me with lies. I witnessed our loss. Reinforcements failed to arrive. Their army marched on, and they killed our people. They killed my son. They killed my GRAND-CHILDREN!"

"Yes, Sir Gibblet. Your forces were defeated by the soldiers of Kraya. They marched on. But you're wrong about the reinforcements. They failed to save you, but they arrived before the city was attacked. Your family was not—"

"DO NOT LIE TO ME, WITCH! I HAVE LIVED—"

"Enough of that," Gam Gam scolded, her voice never rising. The revenant fell silent. "I was talking."

"I will kill you where you stand, old woman."

"Then do it, but you will not learn of your family and their fate." She held out the metal disc, inscribed with the image of a swan in flight over a heart. She felt the gaze of the revenant lock onto the coat of arms and a wave of surprise swarmed around her. The heat cooled in an instant, and her breath returned, as if freed from a wet cloth. A breeze chilled the sweat drenching Gam Gam and sent shivers throughout her body.

Her voice softened with the returned chill. "The reinforcements arrived in time because of your men's sacrifice, Sir Gibblet. The soldiers of Kraya have been paying for their failure for as long as you've been paying for yours. It is time to let go, and to cross the veil. It is time for peace, Sir Gibblet."

"That symbol...my son, he lives?" The voice of the mist cracked with emotion. "My grandchildren?"

"No, they have passed," —the heat returned to the mist, though it lacked its earlier conviction— "*after* having lived long, happy lives. It has been a hundred years, Sir Gibblet. Their lives continued as yours stagnated. But your grandchildren have had children of their own. And those children have grown to have families. The Gibblets are a well-respected family, for what their ancestors have done. Including you."

Gam Gam stepped toward the smoldering eyes, the densest part of the mist. "They lived on thanks to your sacrifice. Your city lived on. You gave them time to muster forces, you gave them a chance to survive, and they did. Your own son took to the battlefield that day, hoping to save you."

"My son..."

"He became the governor after that battle. Shelen prospered greatly under his leadership."

"Oh gods." The revenant pulled into itself, pooling on the ground in front of Gam Gam. "What have I done?" The mist shivered under the weight of the new emotions. Gam Gam reached out. The revenant was cool to the touch.

"You did nothing, it was the revenant. But your spirit is fighting to free itself. I can repair it fully. Return you to what you should have been before the darkness warped you."

"I do not deserve your kindness."

"Everyone deserves kindness, especially those most in pain." Gam Gam brushed the spectral cloud with one hand, as if to provide comfort. "A revenant is formed from powerful emotion at the time of death. Your fear and anger broke your spirit, turned it against who you were. It found a singular focus, an obsession, and you were ruled by it. Until now, when your other emotions have become strong enough to combat those that claimed you. You are in there, Sir Gibblet. The loving, caring knight that you were. Remember the love of your family, and know that they lived. The coat of arms is proof of that. Let your love break you free from your curse, and let me help you the rest of the way."

Gam Gam closed her eyes and the blackness filled her. The strange, nauseating feeling of her necromantic power, like a sludge creeping along her veins. She tugged at the pieces of Sir Gibblet, forming him back into the ghost he should have been. It was not so different from knitting, except instead of yarn it was spectral energy. She pulled on the threads of Sir Gibblet's spirit, looping him together one stitch at a time. The mist followed her motions, and wrapped itself together, condensing into a new form.

The process was slow, and Gam Gam was vulnerable. If the Knight Revenant decided to stay as it was, it could strike her down in a heartbeat. But the only emotion she felt wafting from the ghostly cloud was love and grief.

The spectral energy swirled into the shape of an elderly knight, who dropped to his knees as the spell finished. Newly formed hands rose to his face, covering his eyes. He was balding but for two tufts of hair sprouting above each ear. A long beard hung down over the emblazoned flying swan atop a heart that was the Gibblet coat of arms. Translucent tears fell down his face as he wept, the uncontrollable anger dissipating as his soul reformed.

With some difficulty, Gam Gam lowered herself onto a pair of distressed knees in front of the ghostly knight. She held one hand up to his cheek and hovered there. His fingers parted to reveal cool, gray eyes, anguish replacing the rage that had once burned within. Her heart twisted as he spoke with such pain. "I have killed so many. I almost killed that family. You should have banished me to my torment."

"You cannot change what you cannot control. You have suffered enough, Sir Gibblet. You are not the first revenant, nor did you choose to become one." His eyes dropped away from hers, but she continued. "I offer you a choice. Perhaps it will bring some peace to your heart. You can follow the Call, and cross the Veil of Death. Move to the afterlife you were meant to go to, and see your family once more. Your son, your daughter-in-law, your grandchildren. They wait for you."

"What is the second option?"

"I can soulbind you to me. You will be able to walk this land for as long as I hold the binding, and I will show you everything your sacrifice saved. I will show you the city and how it prospered, the great things your son accomplished. You can see the good you brought to this world. Maybe even find a way to forgive yourself."

The ghost and the necromancer stared at each other for long moments as Sir Gibblet pondered. "If you bind me here, I can still move on to the afterlife? I can still see my family?"

"Any time you wish."

"Then I would like to stay here a little longer. It would be nice to see goodness in this world."

Gam Gam smiled, and again, power filled her. She weaved a thread of necromantic energy between the ghost's soul and her own. Their emotions burned across the binding. Agony and joy warred against each other, and Gam Gam poured her own soothing love into the spirit. "Then I shall show you all I've learned of your family."

Gam Gam struggled to rise, and though Sir Gibblet offered to help, he quickly realized the uselessness of the offer, and stepped back, embarrassed. Instead, the mother raced to Gam Gam's side, and helped her to her feet.

"Thank you very much, dear." Gam Gam brushed the dirt from her skirts and looked to the rest of the family. Parents and children both were red-eyed with tears. She smiled to provide comfort, to tell them that it was done and they were safe. "I can offer you a ride to Shelen if you need it. I do apologize about the donkey, though."

"We would be very grateful for a ride." The woman's eyes sang of hope and relief, and she smiled in return. "Thank you so much for helping us."

"You're very welcome." Gam Gam watched the two children climb out from under the cart—two boys. Not like her family at all. Her mind had played strange tricks on her in the stress of the moment.

"You have my sincerest apologies, as little as they mean to you." Sir Gibblet bowed to the family, tortured grief still fresh across his face. "If it is any consolation, there is very little I can do to harm you in this form."

"We heard everything, Sir," the mother said, "That wasn't you, and you have nothing you need to apologize for. Besides, it was only a frightful scare. No other harm done, right boys?"

The two boys nodded timidly, and the husband confirmed. Though dirty, the family was unharmed. Gam Gam was grateful she was able to make it in time.

"Let's get you to my wagon and we can head into the city," she said.

"Yes, ma'am."

"Now you can knock that off right now. Call me Gam Gam."

"What kind of name is Gam Gam?" the smaller boy asked. His father grabbed the boy's arm and scolded him, but Gam Gam waved him off.

"It's what my grandchildren called me. They're not much bigger than you two. I suppose it's just nice to hear it and remember them."

The family pulled what little they had from the cart and Gam Gam led the way back to her modest, mobile home. It wasn't even three steps before her knees gave out and she fell to the ground in a surprised "Oof."

The mother was by her side in a moment, helping her to her feet. "Thank you dear, but I can walk fine."

"Nonsense, ma—um, Gam Gam. It's the least I can do to help."

Gam Gam grunted, but her knees were thankful for the extra support.

"I'm Therese, by the way," the mother said. "Dale's my husband. The boys, oldest to youngest, are Nolan and Asher."

Gam Gam's heart skipped a beat, and she would have tripped again if not for Therese's help. "Asher?" The name came out in an exhale.

"Yes, named for my father's father."

"That's my grandson's name too."

"Then your grandson has a lovely name."

Gam Gam's thoughts wandered elsewhere, and conversation hushed as the five humans walked (and the one ghost floated) back to the wagon.

Gam Gam drove the wagon through the night as the family slept within. Her knees and hip still ached, but she padded her bench and sat as comfortably as possible while the horses did the hard work. Sir Gibblet, not requiring sleep himself, kept her company for the trek. The two talked about the many things that had happened since the ghost's death, particularly focused on Sir Gibblet's family and home.

By sunrise, the cart reached the city of Shelen. The family said their farewells, giving many thanks and hugs before leaving. Gam Gam's eyes lingered on the youngest boy as they became lost in the crowd.

"We can wait if you need to rest," Sir Gibblet said, but Gam Gam locked up the wagon and hung a little sign on the back that read "MAGE AT WORK. DON'T TOUCH HORSES! THEY EAT FINGERS!" and hoped for the best.

Gam Gam circled around the wagon and pulled a couple of vials of green liquid from her pocket. "Nonsense, Sir Gibblet. I'll hardly be tired at all after one of these. I just bought them from that vendor over there. It's supposed to give you energy. And besides, I'm nearly back to full health." She downed the vial, then her knee betrayed her as she stumbled. Though still sore, the joints *were* working better than before the night had passed. She waved off his worried look, and added, "I'm fine." Then she blinked as wakefulness surged within her. "And that potion certainly works." She pocketed the other vials and headed into town, Sir Gibblet beside her.

The ghostly knight hid himself within the city by growing so transparent only a shimmer remained where he floated. Passing eyes slid around him as though no more than a trick of the light. Though difficult to see, their bond let Gam Gam find the spectral knight at any moment. Emotions and simple thoughts flowed freely between each other. As he grew interested in passing sights, she knew the focus of that wonder.

"It's so different from what I knew," he said.

"A lot changes in a hundred years."

"That inn used to only be one story. Now they're adding a fourth. Are there really so many people in this city?"

"From what I could find, the population has more than tripled since your time. Shelen has prospered because of you."

Gam Gam led him to the town square, the center of which was dominated by a large bronze statue of a similar balding man. Sir Gibblet flew over and studied the statue. Gam Gam took her time weaving through the crowd.

When she arrived, Gibblet looked down at her, and she felt his smile, "It's not a very good likeness, now is it? Looks more like me than how I remember my boy."

"Well, he was significantly older when this was done. It seems he favored his father in looks."

Sir Gibblet laughed, and studied the statue again.

"Come," Gam Gam said. "There's more."

Across the town square, they entered the public lobby of a large government building. Paintings of figures lined the walls. Gam Gam stopped in front of one in particular. "He might be more recognizable here. I believe this was painted closer to the battle, when he was first chosen as governor."

Sir Gibblet stared at the portrait of his son for a long moment. His strong emotions threatened to overwhelm Gam Gam's own, a turmoil of grief and joy. Relief and pain. She let him have the moment to himself.

"Hello again, ma'am. Have you returned for more information?"

A well-dressed young lady walked over to Gam Gam, with her usual practiced smile.

"Oh hello, dear." Gam Gam rubbed at her head. "I know it hasn't been long, but I'm blanking on your name. Could you remind me?" She smiled at her little lie.

"I'm Dalia," she said. If she noticed the faint disturbance beside Gam Gam, she did not show it. "I'm assistant to the governor. I was the one who helped you find some books for your research last time."

"Your full name, dear."

Dalia blinked, caught off guard by the question. "Oh, it's Dalia Gibblet."

Gam Gam smiled at the new emotion. "Like the governor, right?" She pointed to the portrait behind her.

"That's my great-granddad." The practiced smile was replaced with a more radiant, genuine one as Dalia's true passion shined through. "I hope to follow in his footsteps one day, but I doubt I can live up to what he did. To end a war, and bring the city out of its economic spiral. I can't imagine how difficult it was to hold the city together then."

"He sounds like a great man."

"Oh, he was. His father too, both were heroes to this city." Sir Gibblet stiffened at Dalia's words. As much as a ghost can stiffen. "My brother is training to be a knight like him. Perhaps he and I will be the next generation of great

Gibblets." She laughed at her joke, then turned red. She waved a hand in front of her desperately. "Oh, I mean, well I hope I can live up to the name. I don't mean to sound arrogant about it."

"It's fine, dear. It's a worthy goal to strive towards."

"Stories of the brave knight and honorable governor fill our house often. It is truly an honor to have such great ancestors."

"Thank you for sharing with me again, Dalia. You'll be a wonderful governor, I'm sure. I think that's all I need for now." She glanced to the side, and saw Sir Gibblet nod in response. "I'm just looking at the paintings. I'll let you be."

"It was my pleasure, ma'am. Have a wonderful day."

"They still think of me as a hero," Sir Gibblet muttered as he watched his descendant leave.

"You were a hero, Sir Gibblet. The revenant wasn't you."

"I think I understand that now, but I still don't feel like the hero they see me as."

"We cannot control others' perceptions, only our own actions."

"Yes, but I would like to live up to that. Or rather, unlive up to it. You can keep me here for as long as you want, yes?"

"I can, if you wish to stay. But what of your family beyond?"

"They will be there when I'm ready to return, and I think I would like to still bring some good into the world. By your side, I think I can do just that. I still have my honor as a knight, not even death can take that from me."

Gam Gam smiled. "I would love to have the company, Sir Gibblet. You're welcome to stay with me as long as you see fit."

"Then you will have an honorable knight at your side. I am indebted to you." He bowed to her and Gam Gam smacked him on the head. Though her hand went through, Sir Gibblet still jerked away from the maneuver.

"Enough of that," she scolded. "No owing or debts. Let us just be friends."

Sir Gibblet smiled. "Friends we are, then, Gam Gam. Where will we be heading to?"

Gam Gam's smile held firm, but her melancholic emotions betrayed the truth. "To see my family."

Acknowledgments

Gam Gam and Mina wouldn't be here without the help of some magnificent people.

First and foremost, thanks to my wife, Sarah, who has been by my side during my entire writing adventure, and who always believed I could make it this far. She is my first reader, my first editor, and my knitting expert. Anything wrong with the knitting is her fault entirely.

A special thanks to Dylan, a steadfast friend since middle school, and my first confidant after Sarah. I still remember you telling me "You could be a published author," without having read anything I wrote. Thanks for your undying belief that I could do it!

Gam Gam started as a D&D character I thought would be fun to play, if I ever wasn't a forever DM. Fortunately, I mentioned this before I got the chance to play her, and two incredibly special people bullied me into turning her into a story instead. Gam Gam wouldn't be here without the ruthless bullying of Connor and Krystle, so thank you for pushing me down this path and if it weren't for my plans to dedicate my first story to Sarah, this would have been dedicated to the two of you.

Another thanks to Connor for looking over my short story and telling me it needed more room to grow. Your many "!!!!" kept me motivated and excited about what I wrote.

To my early readers, thanks for sticking through the slop and giving advice and comments along the way. Thank you Dan, Dylan, and Jackiie. Your insights were invaluable and helped better my stories.

To my editors, who improved on everything I did, thank you so much. Taya for your commas and clarity and smoothing my words into something far better. And Isabelle for your close attention to detail to smooth the story out, and being able to find some embarrassing mistakes that slipped through everyone else. And, of course, for being the first to ask when you can get your hands on a sequel.

A big shout out to the Swords & Corsets discord server, for letting me fill up the channels with daily accountability threads. Not only did it help me become a more consistent writer, but I became closer to so many great people and have made some wonderful friendships because of it. Special thanks to Angela, Azshure, Connor, Dan, Fiona, Krystle, and Maxime for cheering me on continuously, and for providing many pieces of advice as I figured out this authoring thing.

Endless thanks to those who made Gam Gam look better than I ever could have dreamed possible. Kerstin, I could not have asked for a more perfect illustration to be the face of Gam Gam. I'm lucky to have an immensely talented friend like you to make my book look so good. (Insert bear GIF.) To Virginia, your ability to compliment Kerstin's artwork with the layout is incredible, and the Nugget addition was genius. I screamed about the cover for days after. (I'll be honest, I'm still screaming about it now).

To the many friends I've made through Twitter and Discord, thanks for always cheering me on and making me feel welcome among the indie book community.

And lastly, thank YOU for taking the chance to read this novella about a grandmotherly necromancer and a young girl. I hope you enjoyed your time with Gam Gam and Mina!

Acknowledgments: The Knight Revenant

The more I thought about Gam Gam and Sir Gibblet's relationship, the more I wanted to explore how they met. I had thought it would make a great short story, and even stay as one unlike the original A Necromancer Called Gam Gam, which bloated the constraints of what could be called a short story, then tripled in size. So The Knight Revenant was born.

First and foremost, thanks to my wife, Sarah, who has been by my side during my entire writing adventure, and who always believed I could make it this far. She is my first reader, my first editor, and my knitting expert. Anything wrong with the knitting is her fault entirely.

A special thanks to Dylan, a steadfast friend since middle school, and my first confidant after Sarah. I still remember you telling me "You could be a published author," without having read anything I wrote. Thanks for your undying belief that I could do it!

Thank you to my early readers, who took a peek at a lesser version of this story. Thank you Jackiie for being a big Gam Gam fan and always throwing your support my way in so many different forms. I am eternally grateful to have a publishing buddy like you. And thank you Angela for helping me fix a troublesome spot and making the story better for it.

For my editor, Noah, thank you for improving upon the story and making The Knight Revenant better than I ever could alone.

A big shout out to the Swords & Corsets discord server, for letting me fill up the channels with daily accountability threads. Not only did it help me become a more consistent writer, but I became closer to so many great people and have made some wonderful friendships because of it. Special thanks to Angela, Azshure, Connor, Dan, Fiona, Krystle, and Maxime for cheering me on continuously, and for providing many pieces of advice as I figured out this authoring thing.

Another big thanks to Virginia for pulling together another excellent cover. You constantly make my stories look better, and I appreciate it a ton.

To the many friends I've made through Twitter and Discord, thanks for always cheering me on and making me feel welcome among the indie book community.

And lastly, thank YOU for taking the chance to read this short story about a grandmotherly necromancer helping out the ghost of a knight. I hope you enjoyed your time with Gam Gam!

About Author

Adam Holcombe daylights as a programmer and moonlights as an author. After spending years toying with the idea of writing, he decided to commit and work toward releasing his first novel. Then Gam Gam got in the way, and now he's writing too many stories to count.

When he's not locking himself in a cold basement to type away, he can be found squishing his dog (but not too hard), squawking at his tortoise (but not too loudly), goofing off with his wife (in perfectly ordinary, non-weird ways), playing D&D with friends (I'm playing a character now!), or the usual chilling at home. He is a lover of books, board games, video games, and swords.

Mina and Gam Gam will return in the future, but until then keep your eyes out for the sci-fi novel, Bounty Inc, which will launch a series Adam is very excited to delve into.

Check out bountyink.com for future publishing news, and additional book content.

www.ingramcontent.com/pod-product-compliance
Lightning Source LLC
Chambersburg PA
CBHW030958210726
48290CB00007B/2368